A STORM OF
❧ CHERRIES ❧

BOOKS IN THE SEQUENCE OF
❋ *SONS OF* ❋ *THE MORNING*

VOLUME ONE
A STORM OF ❋ CHERRIES ❋

Sarah –
Happy days at RGS

A STORM OF CHERRIES

SIMON WATSON

WORDWISE
PULBOROUGH • WEST SUSSEX

A STORM OF CHERRIES

• VOLUME ONE OF •

SONS OF THE MORNING

First published in 2006 by
WORDWISE
Brambles, Batts Lane, Pulborough RH20 2ED
Tel: 01798 875413
E-mail: wwordwise@aol.com

ISBN 10 : 0-9553401-0-1
ISBN 13 : 978-0-9553401-0-9

Produced and printed by members of
THE GUILD OF MASTER CRAFTSMEN

Cover Design by Ian Tyrrell
Book Design and Typesetting by Cecil Smith
Typeset in Galliard and Caslon Open Face

Printed and bound in Great Britain by
RPM PRINT & DESIGN
2-3 Spur Road, Quarry Lane, Chichester, West Sussex PO19 8PR

To
My Brothers

❧ A STORM OF CHERRIES ❧

Characters in order of appearance

JOHNNY CLARKE	Protagonist; Head Boy of The Dell
MR VICTOR	Headmaster of The Dell
MR BLACKSTONE	Assistant master
MARVELL	The smallest boy in the school
MR DENMAN	Assistant master
TOM BENNETT	Bottom of the form
HAINES	Johnny's rival
BALMFORTH	Deputy Head Boy
MAJOR OAKES	Assistant master
MRS LOGSDON	Junior class teacher
MR BOLTON	School gardener
EDWARDES	Odd boy
MRS VICTOR	Headmaster's wife
DR WOOLF	Headmaster of Worthington School
MRS MARVELL	Marvell's mother
FLOP	Marvell's pony
GAY PHELPS	Pretty new matron
SINGER SAMUEL	New American boy
GUY STUART-EVERSLEY	Star of Banksfield cricket team
MR HOLLAND	Friend of Mr Victor's
MR SAMUEL	Singer's father

PART ONE

❈ CHAPTER I ❈

Weighing and Measuring was a ritual of the start and end of every term at The Dell. Every boy's height was taken and his weight recorded; in addition, the capacity of his chest for expansion was measured.

As Head Boy Johnny was a functionary at this event, in charge of the contraption that was both scales and, with a tall upright metal bar rising some six feet from its base at the back, a measure of height. It was one of those archaic and over-complicated devices, of which Edwardian store catalogues boasted many, that suggest a function more important or perhaps more sinister than the simple one it actually has. On this instrument Johnny had himself stood twice a term from the age of seven.

'Next!' boomed the headmaster, Mr Victor, from his position at his desk. Before him lay open the book in which boys' vital statistics were recorded for transcription to end-of-term reports. Mr Victor loved trivial and incontestable figures such as batting averages, and put as much time and passion into recording these details of a boy's development as he did into his progress in any academic subject.

Another boy entered the study and began, reluctantly, to undress in a dim corner where two others stood, entirely naked, awaiting their turn. A fourth, the ordeal over, was dressing with dissimulated alacrity.

It was the compulsory nakedness that the boys disliked: postponing till the last moment the removal of the underpants; the shame of attempting to conceal the private parts without actually seeming to be trying to do so; an inchoate but powerful sense of the incongruity between their tender nakedness and the horrible old-mannishness of Mr Victor's study with its pipe-racks, bookcases and faded team photographs; the sheer cold of the instruments of measurement, particularly that of the waxed yellow tailor's tape that Mr Blackstone wrapped round their back for the chest expansion.

'Clarke, did you say "Four foot three and three-sixteenths" or "Four foot three and three-eighths" for Marvell?' Mr Victor enquired.

'Er...' Johnny couldn't for the life of him remember. He glanced, in the hope of thus refreshing his memory, at the small red-haired figure of Marvell now in the taped embrace of Mr Blackstone. 'Three-sixteenths, I think, sir,' he essayed hopefully, knowing Mr Victor disliked dithering. Luckily his answer played straight into the welcoming hands of Mr Victor's relish for sarcasm, one of the unfailing perks of his profession.

'Indeed? In which case young Marvell has shrunk over the Easter holidays. We all know Marvell is small but I don't believe he's shrinking – are you, Marvell?'

'No, sir,' piped Marvell winningly, still within Mr Balckstone's embrace. His role of 'the smallest boy in the school' Marvell ingenuously played to the full. He softened even Mr Victor's hard heart, standing now without self-consciousness, as if he didn't know what nakedness was.

'Better re-measure him, Clarke,' said Mr Victor wearily. 'Come along – get it right first time, we haven't got all day.'

This last was one of Mr Victor's favourite expressions and reflected the hectic life he led as a headmaster who had not only to teach Latin, English, History and Mathematics to the seniors, but also stoke the boiler, order the text books and pay the bills. Amongst other things. He glanced at his watch now, aware that the lawn-mower repair shop would be closing in half an hour and he had not yet begun work on the first eleven wicket, the ancient Atco he possessed for that purpose having failed to come to life after an inactive winter.

'Yes, sir,' said Johnny, irritated at his own failure and distracted by wondering how many other boys' heights he had gauged inaccurately. He felt no indignation at being, as Head Boy, publicly rebuked, for Mr Victor's impatience was a continuous feature of life at The Dell and it fell indiscriminately upon all in his kingdom like Scotch mist. But it dampened Johnny's good spirits.

For one thing this impatience made him aware of how very bad he, in contrast with Mr Victor, was with figures. For as long as he could remember his soul had gone into a kind of spasm at the prospect of numbers, and his lack of numeracy was, as it were, a paralysed left arm that had to be manipulated clumsily by the right arm of his general intelligence and assiduity. The thing with Maths was that as soon as you were perhaps beginning to get the hang of something they moved you on to the next topic which of course you couldn't understand. For another, it drained his confidence in himself as Head of School, reminding him that, hard as he might try to please, he could never apparently succeed in winning Mr Victor's praise. The position of Head Boy presented itself to Johnny less as an accolade or vote of confidence in him on Mr Victor's part than a new opportunity for failure and humiliation.

For Head of School Johnny had not really wanted to be. But then 'I want doesn't get' being a prevalent saw of his upbringing, he had not reflected on it as an option any more than choice came into the matter of which school he attended, what bedroom he had at home, where the family went on holiday and so on. Things happened to him and were as out of his control as the bowling that came at you from the other end: it was all a matter of how you played it when it got to you.

It was anyway unthinkable to say no to what was an honour – indeed the highest honour The Dell had to offer. Other honours such as the captaincies of cricket, hockey and football were already his so there was an easy naturalness in the conferring of the ultimate accolade, just as in the adult world honorary degrees, Companionships of Honour and Orders of Merit, for example, are heaped upon those whose dignities already make it difficult for their complete styling to be contained on a single line of the envelope.

Johnny was one of those whose background and bearing attract promotion. If the chap at least looks and talks right he can't be all wrong as an appointment, can he, however inept he proves to be? – so the unarticulated thinking runs. And Johnny looked and talked right: of slightly above-average height, regular features, blond-brown hair and an impeccable (though by no means patrician) accent. He was a late flowering of the upper echelon of the race that had intrepidly built the largest empire in the history of the world, died patriotically in droves in Flanders and thrashed the Hun from El-Alamein to Normandy and Berlin. Furthermore his father was Rector of the parish in which The Dell was situated. Headmaster and Rector were on good professional and neighbourly terms so what could be more natural than that Johnny should, for his last term, take over as Head of School?

Not but what Mr Victor had had his doubts about the appointment. Of course Mr Victor always had doubts. His deep dissatisfaction with life he fuelled continuously with self-generated disappointments. His perfectionism ensured that he could never be wholly pleased with anyone or accept imperfection as a fact of man's sinful state. To that simplest but deepest of educational tenets that 'boys will be boys' he did, of course, assent; but that they were boys meant that they must undergo a remedial treatment of constant correction so that a proper state of humility and grace might be attained. Thus the native hue of cheerful imperfection amongst the boys was sicklied o'er with the pale cast of Mr Victor's criticism just as it was dampened by the drizzle of his irritability. And his reservations about Johnny centred on the boy's lack of leadership. He had had an unfortunate lapse as dormitory captain not long since and although he had on various fields of play, including the boxing ring, showed plentiful individual pluck – a quality for which Mr Victor had great respect – he was not possessed of true captaincy, that natural self-assurance that drew others towards it and subdued them to its purposes. He was not, for example, to be compared with McPherson, last term's Head of School, who, though not quite the athlete Johnny was, had a quality of control that enabled Mr Victor to relax over those matters of duty and discipline deputed to the Head of School and his prefects. Marlborough would be glad of him.

In truth he was quite right about Johnny, who had no wish to interfere in other people's lives and took no pleasure in command. But the boy was intelligent, decent, hard-working and conscientious, and such qualities were sufficient to attract promotion, particularly where competition was thin. So there he now was on the first day of the summer term with his Head of School badge on his jersey, fully-clothed where others went naked, an official with a job to do while others stood awaiting direction. And already he'd made a bish.

Boys came and went under Johnny's hands. He looked down to determine their weight, up to determine their height. Stone, pounds and ounces; feet and inches. 'If twelve boys in the school weigh between seven and eight stone and there are sixty boys in the school what proportion of the school weighs between eight and nine stone?' Johnny invented the question in exam-paper style. If only the sort of question he would meet in the scholarship exam were that simple. For that was another thing: the scholarship. Even Johnny knew he wasn't expected to win one – indeed an award of any size (and the smallest would have helped his father financially) was thought to be beyond him but Mr Victor, who had both dispiritingly low expectations but relentlessly high aspirations, had persuaded the Rector that his son stood a better chance at Worthington if he offered scholarship rather than Common Entrance papers. And of course it flattered the headmaster's vanity to be doing 'scholarship work' even if his pupil (for Johnny was alone in attempting this challenge) found the work beyond his powers, the problems set even in the easiest of the three Maths papers depriving him of his wits at a glance. He couldn't understand – let alone do – most of them. Trigonometry was quite beyond him. And Mr Victor's response in the face of incomprehension was to force the pace and sharpen his tongue.

Busy as he now was and concentrate hard though he now had to in distinguishing between eighths and sixteenths of an inch, Johnny was able to form more of an impression of the headmaster's study than at any time before. There were in the general way only three reasons for visiting the headmaster's study, one of which was then in operation; the second was for the collection of a new exercise book, and the third was to be beaten. Mr Victor regarded the request for a new exercise book as an act of irresponsibility and greed. The dog-eared article allegedly 'full' would be proffered to Mr Victor with trepidation. Mr Victor took it as something dirty but inevitable before flicking through it to ascertain that it really was 'full' – which in his eyes it rarely was, for was not here, towards the beginning, a quarter of a page in which a sum of moderate size might be worked? – and here – look – were several lines sufficient to accommodate a short spelling test. And what was the objection to writing on the inside covers? Such spaces would be firmly and blackly pencilled off and the full-book applicant would retreat, convicted of waste, with the same dog-eared volume. Mr Victor hated waste more than anything. But he was not a great beater. Such offences as stealing and cheating must of course be punished with 'the cane' but as Johnny had never stolen or cheated he had never been beaten.

Nonetheless the Headmaster's study was a dreaded place. No august room, it did not intimidate by size or grandeur, being a garret room (originally a servant's bedroom) with sloping ceilings and dormer windows with no outlook. It was with its quality of an eyrie stuffed with the appurtenances of a middle-aged pedagogue that it appalled. It contained heavy glass-fronted bookcases of volumes, mostly in sets, of indecipherable title: they were dark blue and thick. There was nothing of comfort except a deep leather easy chair across whose frayed arm a chromium ash-tray sat, held in safety in that otherwise unstable position by a leather strap threaded through its base and weighted with lead sewn into either end, for Mr Victor was a great pipe-smoker, as the pipe-racks and distinctive smell of the man and his room redolently testified. It was over the other side of this chair that the beaten, trouserless, were obliged to bend, their noses thereby coming repellently close to the offensive ash-tray.

The room was dominated by a large central desk, covered with exercise books, invoices and more ash-trays. Elsewhere was further pedagogic clutter – an ancient wooden filing cabinet, cricket stumps, a bag of boxing gloves, an old globe etc. Mr Victor being, as observed, a hater of waste threw nothing away, for what as yet unforeseen use might not be found for a set of Hillard and Botting so coverless, stained and torn as to be no longer usable even at The Dell? The room's other dominant feature in normal times was the weighing and measuring contraption that Johnny was at present privileged to be operating. Normally it stood in a dim corner like some sort of miniature guillotine in reserve. Mr Victor's study was a dark and alien place, total in its power over any boy who entered it.

'That's the last one, Headmaster,' said Mr Blackstone when there seemed to be no further naked wretches to submit to the embrace of his chilly tape.

'Good,' said Mr Victor. 'Clarke, give me a hand with this' – 'this' being the guillotine – 'Thank you for your help, Mr Blackstone. Oh! – we haven't done you, have we, Clarke?'

'Er, no, I don't think we have, sir.' Of course they jolly well hadn't. The prospect of stripping like the others had been another of those things – along with Mr Victor and the smell of his pipe, the burden of his office and the difficulty of scholarship papers – that had been sapping his cheer throughout his operation of the guillotine. Mr Blackstone paused, hopefully retaining the tape.

'Well, just slip off your shoes and jersey – no need to strip down. And we'll dispense with chest expansion. Thank you, Mr Blackstone.' Mr Victor took the tape from his assistant master's hand a little brusquely.

Mr Victor hated not doing things properly but he had to get that mower; it was such inevitable compromises as this that lent edge to his irritation. And besides he wanted a word with his new Head of School. Johnny stepped on to the instrument in his own turn. Mr Victor was horribly close to him so that Johnny received his tobaccoy exhalations without dilution.

'Keep them all in order,' he commanded. 'Put a stop to any trouble before it gets out of hand. Make sure the prefects do their duties – and I look to you to keep me in touch with what's going on.' This last injunction Mr Victor never omitted from this particular 'chat' even though heads of school were unswerving in their reluctance to share any more than they absolutely had to with their headmaster. 'And remember – you can always come to me when you need any advice... help... that sort of thing.' A nauseating blast accompanied this final enjoinder so that Johnny's 'Thank you, sir' as he was given permission to leave the room was hard to articulate but deeply felt in the relief of escaping the man and his tobacco-breath and the guillotine and the study. The staircase outside the study Johnny descended by means of sliding down the banisters – a mode of travel common if somewhat infra-dig on the part of the Head of School – and concluded with a joyous flourish of the legs.

A few moments later Mr Victor, a good job done, took the same descent though in more adult manner, his heavy brown brogues meeting each tread with familiar authority but Johnny was too far away for his poor heart to sink at the sound.

❈ CHAPTER II ❈

The Dell was, with fewer than sixty boys, still a viable prep-school by the standards of the time. Most of them were boarders, a very few were day-boys and none were in that (to Mr Victor) despicably hybrid category: the weekly boarder. It was situated on the outskirts of a small town in the home counties from which most of the adult male inhabitants travelled up to London every day by train.

The house itself had been built as a gentleman's residence – somewhat more than a villa and something less than a mansion – but was of little age and no architectural merit. Mr and Mrs Victor had bought it with their small savings and a legacy immediately after the war. They had ambitions for their school and set about converting the house with determination. In no time a paddock became a playing-field, the larder a lavatory, the bedrooms dormitories and so on, though plenty of outhouses and so forth had yet to be improved. Being a new establishment, however, the school did not at once attract customers of the highest class. The locality was dotted with the homes of stock-brokers and what Mr Victor referred to generically and not without contempt as ' businessmen', but these men of wealth and family patronised other establishments, many of them miles away, that prepared the boys for transition to the grander public schools. It was true that one father of a boy at The Dell had a Daimler but some parents had no car at all and paid the fees in cash. Most of the boys came from families of modest professional, commercial and clerical status; several were the sons of war-widows on pensions and some were actually shop-keepers. Mr Victor always aspired to raise the social calibre of his intake but could do nothing to redress his first mistake: setting the fees too low in order to attract parents at the outset. What these low fees did attract was the less well-off and those of no social pretension. To raise the fees now, however, Mr Victor reasoned with himself (for he had none to advise him) would be to risk losing his lower middle class clientele without any firm hope of attracting the upper middle class.

In this long hard clamber up the social rockface Johnny was a modest help to Mr Victor. Being the son of the Rector he was better than the son of a draper. Besides, his father kept, Mr Victor knew, quite lofty company which might be drawn to The Dell by Mr Clarke's recommendation of it. McPherson's award at Marlborough was another step up so some progress was being made.

But if the calibre of his clientele was a source of dissatisfaction to Mr Victor that of his staff was even more so. For good staff did not exist: such quality as the teaching profession might contain did not want to teach in a preparatory school. Mediocre staff were hard to find and, in his experience anyway, hard to retain. Even poor staff were not abundant. The staff at The Dell in its five-year history comprised the aged and the injured, the widowed and the odd. Mr Victor saw himself as the central upright post round which these feeble and faltering growths needed to twine.

One thing Mr Victor had quickly learned about staff recruitment: not to enquire deeply into an applicant's background. This was not so much because such enquiry led to skeletons in cupboards as because the applicant invariably, when obliged to confront his own poor past, resorted to evasiveness, boastfulness or – Mr Victor often suspected – sheer mendacity. Better not ask – if the man did not offer – what he had done in the war or which university (if indeed any) he had attended; better assess the man on the spot and hope for the best. Anyway it was surprising how often the ability to handle a lawn-mower could sweep away reservations.

Of Mr Blackstone, for example, Mr Victor knew very little. The man had spent some time in Paris before the war (not promising, that), though in what capacity Mr Victor could not now remember, if he had indeed ever known. He was clearly intelligent and willing and the boys liked him. Handle a lawn-mower he could not but as the only applicant for the post of French teacher – apart from a Belgian widow with a hairy chin and a heavy accent whom the boys would murder within a week – he was clearly acceptable in spite of something in his dress and manner that struck Mr Victor uneasily as a little odd in an indefinable way. In the event it had turned out that his classes were in order – he had a waspish tongue when required – he did his duties amiably and took rabbits football without complaint if with little knowledge of the rules of the game.

Mr Denman had lost half an arm in the war but was nonetheless a very masculine person with a commanding presence, pedagogic authority and a gift with carburettors. He covered Science for the Sixth Form (of which more in a moment), Maths for the juniors, Drawing, and, in spite of his disability, the woodwork shop and model-making. He roused at anything under fifty in a skirt but such were few and – often because of him – transient. In class he would follow any red herring but had a violent temper, the threat of which kept the boys at bay.

Johnny sat before him now. It was a Science lesson and it took place where the sixth formers had all their lessons – in the dining room. This room was the largest in the house containing three long tables which, with members of staff (Mr Victor centrally) at their heads, accommodated all the school. Food arrived on a large three-decker trolley conducted skilfully by a prefect and was dispensed therefrom – the blackboard having been folded up and lent against the jam cupboard – by Mrs

Victor who could calculate down to a single potato how much should go on each plate. All must partake, though 'a small' was permitted, and no food must be left. On the mantel-piece stood an array of shining trophies, several of them deriving from other schools now defunct and testifying to prowess in sports The Dell did not offer. Thus on Sports Day the winner of the 440 yards race might be presented with a trophy previously given elsewhere for .22 shooting or the Senior Paperchase.

Mr Victor hated novelty in any sphere but particularly in the educational. He would have resisted the introduction into the syllabus of such modern subjects as History and Geography ; indeed would probably have opposed the use of the printing press had he been professionally active at the time of its invention. But The Dell must compete and therefore it must conform where necessary. Thus, although Science had first been taught in England some century previously, it was only now being instituted as a subject at The Dell in accordance with a growing educational requirement: there was now a Science paper in the scholarship and C.E.exams. The decision to implement this, however, was not fully matched by the means with which to do so. The school had no laboratory or equipment of any kind and no textbooks. At a practical level Biology might have been attempted by resort to the flora and fauna in the school grounds but Mr Denman had neither knowledge of nor feeling for plants and animals. On the blackboard and with some coloured chalks which had been issued to him as an extravagant teaching aid necessitated by his new subject Mr Denman attempted to explain about the atom, the splitting of which had had such momentous consequences for their era.

This was hard to follow. However, as another extravagance, the boys had all been issued with a brand-new exercise book on whose stiff front cover each had proudly inscribed the bold term: **Science**. The liberality of their issue was a wonder in itself, enriched by the fact that they were in a new colour – beige – thereby increasing the range of text-book colours (orange for Maths, green for Geography etc.) The boys handled these articles with pleasurable awe, reluctant to soil their virgin sheets with anything so clumsy as their own version of Mr Denman's version – in itself far from accurate – of the composition of an atom.

Fortunately for teacher and taught it was clearly understood that while the new subject was now firmly part of the syllabus – as prospective parents were informed – no papers would be sat in the subject that year. Science need not therefore be taken seriously and after the initial assault upon the concept of the atom the old question that never failed – 'Sir, tell us about your Centurion' – ensured pleasurable indolence for the boys as Mr Denman illustrated (coloured chalks useful here too) and discoursed about the tank in whose operation in North Africa he had lost the bottom half of his left arm.

Johnny titivated the cover of his exercise book and reflected on his job as Head Boy after twenty-four hours in the role. He could see there was going to be trouble. In the dormitory for a start. Mr Victor, for reasons of staff convenience disguised as proper concern for boys' health of body and mind, believed not only in bed at an early hour but also in rest after lunch. The latter meant that boys were supposed to be resting when they were most inclined to be active, and the former – in summer anyway – that there were fully two hours of daylight after 'lights out'. Both these conditions made for trouble – trouble it was the responsibility of the dormitory captain, of whom tremendous powers of individual and crowd control were implicitly expected by the higher authorities, to scotch, so that the staff, thus relieved of front-line supervision, were free to have their after-lunch coffee or to read the paper in peace.

Johnny had suffered and seen others suffer in this role before; witnessed the collapse of nice straightforward boys into brutal tyrants or cringing sycophants in their desperate attempts to reconcile the conflicting roles of companion amongst equals and officer set in authority over them as the boys waited for sleep. Many were the recourses adopted in the attempt to while away the tedious hours of enforced inactivity: talking – endless talking; story-telling and singing at the more peaceful end of the scale, with victimisation, bed-hopping, pant-flicking and pillow-fighting at the rowdier end – though it was over none of these that Johnny had dramatically demonstrated his unsuitability for true captaincy but in an unusual manner.

There had been in his dormitory a boy called Tom Bennett who was as practically skilled as he was academically inept. Tom could make most things and mend anything. While any boy could make a torch out of a bulb and a battery Tom could make one with a lens, a switch and a case out of the most everyday or chance materials. His tuck-box was crammed with bits and pieces out of which his technological marvels were worked. Unfortunately, as one who valued every object as grist to his mill, not all the trifles he snapped up were as unconsidered as they should have been: he failed to distinguish, as Mr Victor put it in his post-corporal-punishment oration, betwen 'meum' and 'tuum'. Now Tom was a great collector of keys and in this collection was one which fitted the sweet cupboard, the absolute security of which was of vital importance to everyone.

It was the practice that each boy brought back to school at the beginning of term a quantity of sweets in a tin. This tin was instantly handed over to the possession of Matron, marked by her in her reassuringly rounded hand with the owner's name, and deposited in the sweet cupboard. To hold back any part of the tin's contents for consumption in legally unspecified quantities and at an unlawful time was morally unthinkable. The law laid down – in appropriate reinforcement of the rationing then nationally in effect – that each boy might have two sweets from his tin after lunch every other day, with three on Saturday and Sunday. Matron was the ultimate arbiter of how many sweets a Mars bar, for example, might be defined as comprising, and her ruling, though occasionally if hopelessly contested by the consumer, was always upheld, partly through strength of her own ample personality, partly through pressure from those in the queue behind whose enjoyment of their own sweets was being delayed by the litigant.

Now it so happened that this sacred cupboard – a capacious affair built into the wall and intended originally perhaps for linen – was situated inside the dormitory of which Johnny was captain and the key-collecting Tom Bennett one of the inmates. Tom was into the cupboard before Johnny could even assess his responsibilities in the matter so that it was very soon the nightly practice that all members of the dormitory supplemented their post-lunch sweets with another one or two – not so many, of course, that Matron might possibly notice and they were always careful to leave their stacked tins as they found them and to dispose of the wrappers with care. This arrangement proceeded satisfactorily for some time but enterprise always seeks to improve upon itself and it was an easy transition from raiding one's own supply to raiding other people's – initially under the prompting of curiosity – 'no harm in looking' – which rapidly degenerated to downright theft. Then guilt and quarrelling set in. Some would not steal, others stole reluctantly, while yet others stole with easy rapacity. Johnny (a non-stealer) felt increasingly uncomfortable, ineffectually urging restraint but unable to stem the felonious tide. Dolefully he chewed on his own one or two sweets while the unwitting possessors of crammed tins were steadily plundered. Of course it went too far; of course suspicions arose. These suspicions naturally centred on the inhabitants of the dorm generally and the crafty Bennett in particular. One night a key-hole watch was mounted and as the customary pillage got under way Mr Denman burst in and caught them red-handed.

Moral turpitude of many facets they swiftly learned themselves to be guilty of. Mr Victor was unsparing in his denunciations of their thievery, dishonesty, greed and – worst of all – betrayal of trust. Those in whose dormitory the sweet-cupboard was situated should have seen its existence there as prompting guardianship not looting. And as for the dorm captain ... words failed Mr Victor at Johnny's dereliction of duty: not only deliberately abrogating his responsibility for others but actually participating in the crime. For such a crime mere beating would seem routine and inadequate: nothing less than the enveloping of the entire dormitory in the thickest cumulonimbus of Mr Victor's disapprobation, with (of course) loss of sweet privileges, 'hard labour' and early bedtimes, would suffice to make plain to sinners and innocent alike the full extent of the offence. Johnny was demoted as dormitory captain, his place taken by an ineffectual boy whose want of character it was safe to assume would not be put to the test by his dorm mates during their period of moral exile. As for Tom Bennett, Mr Victor was tempted to take the opportunity of expelling a boy whose craftiness – his father was engaged in trading in a variety of materials and commodities and paid the fees in cash from his back pocket – coupled with his irremediable want of academic ability and intellectual endeavour made him a liability to The Dell. It would have been an impressive demonstration of strength and moral principle 'pour encourager les autres', but consideration of fees prevailed and Tom Bennett remained – albeit the keys of his tuck box confiscated.

But that was in the past. Johnny's new dormitory posed other problems that promised to be just as difficult. No time for them now: the first Science lesson of his life was just ended and Mr Victor had replaced Mr Denman at the blackboard and he was writing as follows:

✳ CHAPTER III ✳

'Although the boy could do the sum if he put his mind to it he decided that since he had always been told to ask more questions in class he would seek his master's advice when the opportunity arose.'

There it was – a juicy complex sentence: if Science offered no opportunity for dissection English certainly did. Of all the work in English Mr Victor liked parsing best: he was an absolute master of English grammar; he revelled in the posing of problems to which authoritative solutions could be found; and his pupils' ignorance of and reprehensible indifference to this branch of the rhetorical craft afforded him many opportunities for justified impatience and sarcastic scorn. He took his chair in comfortable expectation of an enjoyable hour. 'Line up,' he then called.

With very different expectations did the twelve boys who comprised the Sixth and Upper Fifth respond. Each with the grey exercise book in which he had written the sentence filed out from the dining table and positioned himself in front of Mr Victor, like a firing squad in reverse. 'The order is, first: McPherson – no, of course, he is no longer with us – Clarke first, Haines second, Balmforth third, Russell-Jones fourth...'

and so Mr Victor went on to order the line, this order being the status quo ante at the end of the previous term. 'The line' constituted an important element in Mr Victor's pedagogic method: the class, ranged in order of merit, were questioned individually on points relating to the subject matter in hand, the top of the line first. If the top man answered correctly then he retained his position and was unassailable, the next question being directed at the man below him, and so on. If, however, he failed to answer correctly then the second man might do so; if *he* were right then he would change places with number one and so become top of the line. Failure on his part as well as number one's gave to number three the opportunity for promotion direct to number one – and so on down the line so that theoretically number twelve could become number one with a single word should all eleven of his antecedents fail with it. This unlikely event had once been known to happen when an inspired dullard had hit on the right answer and so been propelled to glory. Like an overweight quarter-master suddenly leading an attack under enemy fire he felt intensely uncomfortable at the top which he knew to be the rightful place of the scholars and rapidly sank down the line again until he was restored to the low level to which nature had called and Mr Victor assigned him. Generally, however, the question never got as far as number twelve for Mr Victor would be unable to contain his impatience and would himself shoot out the correct answer at some floundering ignoramus at about number six.

The line having been properly ordered – the boys would be expected to remember it in future – the next operation was to engage in a little random sniping and catch a few dunderheads on matters of spelling and punctuation – it was wonderful how many boys could get such things wrong even in the process of simple copying – before proceeding to the richer work of close analysis. So: 'Haines, spell "opportunity" .' Haines read from his book; he could have read the word from the blackboard but that was not the point and he wouldn't have dared. Haines got it right. 'Bennett – if "seek" is a verb , which I think you will agree it is, what is its noun form?' A tricky question, guaranteed to defeat the boy in spite of its having arisen the previous term. Silence. Bennett shuffles. 'Oh, for heavens' sake, "search", Bennett, "search".' Bennett (limply): 'Yes, sir.' Clearly the permanent number twelve took 'search' from Mr Victor's lips to be an exhortation to further mental effort on his part rather than the answer to the question. Mr Victor groaned histrionically and clapped a despairing hand to his brow. 'Put him out of his misery, Clarke.' Johnny obliged, uncomfortably: the only way to put Bennett out of his misery would be to let him go away and mend a wireless. Unfortunately, Mr Victor reflected, even so lowly and 'progressive' a public school as that to which the boy was destined did not include knowledge of radio-electronics amongst its admission requirements. Poor Tom was ineradicably placed at the bottom of the line; frequently he attempted no answer and Mr Victor simply swept by him; almost invariably he got it wrong – after all, if those above him had failed how on earth could he be expected to succeed? He had got it right once, however, with a Latin test answer – quite fortuitously chosen – of 'erat'. Tom attempted the occasional reiteration of that word, both in faint hope of its repeated success and as if to demonstrate to Mr Victor, however lamely, that it was not quite all up with him in the great academic race. 'Oh, Nebbett, what shall we do with you?' groaned Mr Victor, this sobriquet of his own invention deriving from the bearer's habit of transposing letters in writing in a perverse manner and sometimes when the correct version of the tortured word was before his very eyes – a habit Mr Victor found quite peculiarly irritating.

Now to meatier matters: 'Clarke, of course you know which the concessive clause is?'

'Yes, sir. "Although the boy could do the sum…" '

'Correct. And the causal clause?'

'The causal clause… there isn't one, sir – I don't think.'

'You don't think?'

'There isn't one, sir.'

'Quite so. Now in that concessive clause how would you define the word "could"? '

'It's an auxiliary verb, sir.'

'Yes, an auxiliary... a modal auxiliary.'

It was rare for a correct answer to be, in Mr Victor's eyes, both fully and absolutely correct. He turned from Johnny to number two with a hint of reluctance, as a bowler will conclude an unfruitful over he knows to have been a good one, leaving the undeserving batsman at his crease.

'Haines, what is the main clause?'

This was frequently a trickier one than it seemed – surely the main clause would offer itself up? By no means always so for often it was oddly positioned or divided in two or – as in the present case – very short. Silence and a hard concentrated look from Haines. Mr Victor's brogue began to swing in pleasurable anticipation of more awkward silences, perhaps a few ripe blunders and then opportunities for sarcasm.

Haines: '...he would seek – '

Mr Victor: 'No. Balmforth?'

Balmforth: (Silence).

Number four did no better, by which time collective intellectual resignation had set in and the question ran the length of the line, barely pausing with bemused Nebbett, to fetch up at last with Johnny whose clear 'he decided' settled the matter.

A satisfactory atmosphere of ignorance, shame, fear, academic indifference and latent resentment having thereby been established, Mr Victor's lesson limped on through the remainder of its grammatical constituents to its close with the setting for prep of an essay entitled 'Harvest'.

Particularly when he had got right the question about the main clause that Haines had got wrong Johnny felt uncomfortably aware of that boy's presence at his elbow. In fact, on and off, he had always been uncomfortably aware of Haines. They were class rivals (although Johnny had the edge and Haines was not attempting a scholarship), fellow opening bowlers and in a sense friends. But Haines was tight-skinned and bony-featured, nimble and hard-hearted. When they met with boxing gloves on there was a look in Haines' eye that said 'Victory before Friendship'. Johnny feared him, now more than ever that he was Head of School, which perhaps Haines had hoped to be.

The dormitory trouble that Johnny had feared soon surfaced and Haines was the ring-leader.

The senior dorm was on the ground floor, a spacious room with two-sided aspect and large – hitherto uncurtained – windows, the boys adjusting to daylight at ten p.m. and again at five a.m. in the summer. Now, to the amazement of all the inmates, curtains had been fitted. These were long, red and of some material that owed little to nature, one feature of it being that it was rather hairy, which is to say that a large number of thin, curly synthetic filaments stood out from the main weave. Dorm occupants were naturally intrigued by this hirsute outgrowth and ran hands and faces along it for the pleasure of the soft tickling.

But Haines had made another discovery, for Haines had a box of matches. Now possession of matches was against school rules, the use of them a major offence. Haines was not one to get into trouble – he had after all been appointed a school prefect – but he did often generate it. As now.

By simple experimentation Haines – plus admiring crowd – discovered that each protruding filament would, at the application of a lighted match, flame momentarily as it writhed and shrivelled down to the main body of the cloth, at which point the flame went out without apparently threatening to ignite anything else. This inflammatory discovery led to another, greater. The lit filament flamed – though very briefly – long enough to set light to its neighbour above. That passed the flame upwards in turn so that a small single ignition at the base of the curtain resulted in a climbing streak of flame that ultimately and instantly expired without damage at the curtain rail. It was a thrilling sight.

Johnny was still in the bathroom when this enterprising diversion was first happened upon. By the time he reached the dormitory it was well under way and the entire complement was rapt with excitement as Haines (sole controller of the matches) master-minded his display. There was no question of 'putting a stop to it' before it 'got out of hand' – it had already, as was clear from the gleam in the eye of the spectators, 'got out of hand'. Besides, Johnny was at first equally entranced by the astonishing spectacle.

A further improvement to it was being put into effect just as Johnny arrived: instead of a single match being used to start a thin aspiring train of flame it was planned to light four matches at once and apply them simultaneously a foot or so apart to the skirts of the curtain, creating thereby some sixty square feet of apparent inferno.

'Ready? Go!' Haines' commanding tone.

There was a scraping and the spurt of flame, a momentary pause and then the leaping of fire. From where Johnny stood – well away by the door – it was as if the curtain had indeed burst into flame and although this flaming lasted no more than two seconds it was an alarming sight. Johnny, alone in his pyjamas, his sponge-bag dangling from his hand, knew he must not let this go on.

'What do you think of this, Clarke?' called out an eager onlooker.

'Pretty amazing, but I don't think we should do any more.'

Nobody attended to him as they moved hurriedly on to the next curtain and huddled in readiness for a ring-side seat at the next quadruple firing. Up it went again, this time less gratifyingly.

'We're running out of whiskers on this curtain. Better move on to the next one.' And there was another general scramble for positions of vantage at the neighbouring window.

'Haines, can *I* have a go?'

'*I* haven't done one yet.'

Their attention briefly abstracted from the firing, Johnny

made another attempt.

'Come on, you lot, you know that's dangerous.'

'It's all right, it only burns the little hairy bits.'

'Yes, and it doesn't leave any black marks or anything.'

'Honestly, Clarke, it hardly even makes a pong.'

None of these defensive voices was that of Haines himself and this angered Johnny who knew that the boy with his back turned quietly preparing for the next firing was the real mover.

'Haines, I think you'd better stop,' said Johnny in clear tones.

'It's not doing any harm,' was the muted reply.

'You know you're not supposed to have matches anyway.'

'Just one more,' Haines asserted rather than requested and eager conspirators gathered round him in hope of being elected match-holders.

Once more, the gratifying curtain of flame.

'All right, that's it for tonight, folks,' said Haines jocularly, moving away from the scene, unlawful matches in hand.

'Oh, go on, Haines – there's still plenty to do.'

'No, we don't want them all used up in one session, do we? – got to leave some for another time.'

So they were stopping – that was something, and, Johnny realised, because he had said so. But it was clear from Haines' words that that was not to be the last of the curtain burnings. He might be obeying Johnny now but in the longer term he would do what he wanted. Johnny's soul writhed within him in instinctive revulsion against a power greater than his own.

'I'll take the matchbox, Haines,' he said. He did not expect Haines to submit to so humiliating a confiscation and was a little surprised when the box was tossed roughly in his direction. But the box was empty. 'The matches too.'

'Here they are,' called Haines cheerily and he held out his hand to display them in his palm.

What should Johnny do? Wait to be brought them or see what Haines would do next? He made the mistake of approaching. Just as he reached out to take them he realised what Haines had in mind – to throw them up in the air and then leave Johnny to grovel on the floor for them. But with a quick spurt of rage Johnny grabbed hold of his wrist before he could do that and in no time they were fighting – silently and violently.

'Fight! Fight!' went up the gleeful cry.

Johnny and Haines toppled on to a bed which crashed into the bed next to it, Johnny wrenching at his opponent's closed fist.

But not for long. Matron was at the door and her stillness put a stop to it. Johnny and Haines – a moment before bitter combatants – were now instantly united in the pretence that they had just been ragging. Without making any remark about their being supposed to set an example in their positions, Matron succeeded in making them feel like silly little boys. Fortunately, distracted by this fracas, she did not notice the matches.

After 'lights-out' – i.e. the famous curtains had been drawn by improbably eager volunteers suddenly anxious lest Matron get close enough for suspicion – there was an uncertain mood in the dorm. Johnny had been a 'spoil-sport' – no doubt of that. On the other hand he had risked getting into trouble himself over the fighting when he could have told Matron all and got Haines into serious trouble – and he hadn't done so; there was something decent about that.

For his own part Johnny reflected that in history battles were generally designated a defeat for one side and a victory for the other. Didn't they ever have draws?

✻ CHAPTER IV ✻

W hen not in class Mr Denman would stalk around the school mending things or fly into a rage and throw chisels across the carpentry shop. Not so Mr Blackstone who was not only much more equable in temper but also wholly unpractical. His extra-curricular commitment was of a more social and sedentary nature – taking detention, for example, or playing the piano for the entertainment of the boys as they lined up for lunch. He could take games but, while Mr Denman would change into shorts and run about with a whistle on a proper pitch, Mr Blackstone, largely ignorant of the rules governing any sport, was consigned to a more remote triangular corner of the junior playing field, thick with tussocks of coarse grass, where, placing his feet carefully so as not to spoil with damp his snuff suede oxfords, he would exhort a small and mostly unwilling band of 'rabbits' with inspiriting cries, using his whistle more as a sort of tally-ho than as a means of drawing the players' attention to some significant moment of play. Much of the short time given to these games – and short it was, for changing into the right kit and making their way without deviation or undue dawdling to the designated field of play could be a lengthy procedure for the seven-year-olds – was taken up with minor or imaginary injuries and accusations of foul play which were entirely ignored.

Also, by way of contrast, while Mr Denman occupied a small

attic room in the school – his only home in the world – Mr Blackstone (also unmarried) lived, in circumstances unknown, in the town. It was he, however, who provided a quality of homeliness of which the boys were generally starved. It was not Mr Denman's way, nor that of the taciturn Major Oakes, the other living-in member of staff who, together with Miss Logsdon, the teacher of the bottom form (both hitherto unmentioned) comprised the teaching strength of The Dell – it was not their way to provide much pastoral or personal nourishment. But Mr Blackstone, though accorded little more than the closed-off end of a corridor as his room in school, was ceaselessly hospitable and when off duty was At Home there – as a formal invitation card pinned to his door proclaimed – to any boy who cared to come. Many did and often.

There – and there alone for they were otherwise prohibited – comics (supplied at Mr Blackstone's personal expense) might be read; there one might do a jigsaw puzzle (the pieces missing carefully notified on the front of the box), play games of cards or board games like Ludo and Snakes and Ladders; there one might read volumes with titles like *The Wonder Book of Ships* or – the most popular volume with the greatest number of 'After You's' attached to it – *The Book of Comic and Curious Facts* which recorded such things as the number of doughnuts once consumed at a sitting by a farmer's boy in Oklahoma or how many nuts and bolts there were in the Clifton Suspension Bridge. Drinking chocolate also was served from time to time and music frequently played, for Mr Blackstone possessed a gramophone and numerous records catering for youthful tastes: the greatest number of requests was for *The Blue Danube* and *The Laughing Policeman*.

Such pleasures created for the boys an oasis in a desert of discipline and dull work. Some boys, of course, came more than others. The younger ones were the most constant patrons, going in nightly in dressing gown and slippers before bed. Of these none was more constant or more – it seemed – at home than young Marvell.

Now for Johnny as Head of School the casual and levelling atmosphere of Mr Blackstone's room was not appropriate and he took instead – as do many who seek escape from the burdens of office – to gardening. The grounds at The Dell were extensive, comprising woodland where trees might be climbed, overgrown shrubberies wherein camps might be made and untended paddocks where butterflies might be chased. Hours of free time in summer did the boys spend simply 'outside'. But at the end of a tiring day of lessons, cricket, inspecting fifty or so pairs of hands for cleanliness before lunch and supper, supervising prep and so forth Johnny's soul was pleasantly calmed by tending his small patch.

The school gardener, a morose and ineffectual man called Bolton, had, as instructed, grudgingly accorded to Johnny a small strip of the walled kitchen garden that was his principal private domain. Relics like the knotted remains of a long since barren espalier pear tree against one wall, a leaf-curled peach-tree on another, a near-glassless greenhouse, box hedges died or gone hopelessly leggy, all testified to the former horticultural grandeur of the place and its current neglect. A small shanty town of sheds and lean-tos in one corner housed such tools and equipment as Mr Bolton had command of and provided such space as was needed for the little potting that he did. Before this shanty a patch of cultivated ground nurtured annuals for planting into the one or two beds around the school that were Mr Bolton's principal care, supplemented by a pair of old wooden wheelbarrows that were planted up and put in place on the lower lawn for Sports Day. He grew no vegetables, having at an early stage demonstrated incontrovertibly to the Victors, hopeful of trug-loads of fresh greens for the boys, the hollowness of such a dream by making no attempt, having grudgingly sown the seed, to deter the numerous predators from carrot-fly to pigeons that descended from all quarters to savage the first signs of the wholesome growth that even Mr Bolton's hatred of nature could not entirely prevent from springing up.

The garden was strictly out-of-bounds and great was the wrath of Mr Bolton if he encountered any member of the school trespassing there – a naturalist, perhaps, drawn to the possibilities in the water-tanks, or a forager in hope of some form of sustenance. In fact, of course, Mr Bolton not working in the evening, it was easy to invade in search of tart green gooseberries – a few bushes of great age remained and fruited – but generally the 'out-of-bounds' interdiction lay effectually upon the place and even Johnny, officially permitted to do so, felt some discomfort at entering and working in the garden. This, however, made it all the more attractive as a place of escape, for Johnny could be confident he would not be interrupted. As he worked he listened to the cries of his fellows beyond the high red-brick walls as they played 'It' in the woods, climbed trees, raided one another's camps and persecuted the weak. He felt a little guilty – as Head of School should he not be everywhere all the time, like God? – but this guilt nourished the lonely pleasure of his innocent and privileged pastime. The surrounding wall was as a fortress enclosing him, though at times he felt vulnerable there and the ordinary everyday cries of the boys beyond seemed like the war-cries of a dangerous tribe mustering for action beyond the palisades.

It being a private place and out-of-bounds, Johnny was surprised to find another boy in the garden when he went there unusually early one evening. Against the wall, in a dank gap between the end of a crumbling wooden shed and a large water-tank, Edwardes had set up his altar: a stone block of unknown former function, on which he had erected a bamboo cross of his own manufacture. Johnny was at first naturally reluctant to interrupt the kneeling figure evidently deep in prayer but, having waited and watched a little while, he did so.

'What are you doing, Edwardes?'

'I'm praying for the heathen, my enemies,' came the reply.

'What enemies?'

'*Them!*' Edwardes enunciated violently, stabbing a sharp forefinger in the direction of the sounds of playing boys.

'Who is 'them'?' Johnny persisted.

'*All* of them – Haines and people – they won't leave me alone. They call me names.'

Johnny knew this was true. Edwardes was one of those boys who is picked on because he was 'odd'. He had wild black curly hair and a frenzied look in his eye. He prayed out loud in the dormitory at night and seemed to have no aptitude whatever for the simple rough-and-tumble of childhood. He could not bear to be teased and then put himself in the wrong by retaliating violently. On the games field he participated as little as possible; when eventually coerced into a tackle he would launch a violent and vicious assault upon his opponent and then become aggrieved at being disciplined for it. He had no sense of humour or proportion and no friends. He was desperately untidy in his work – in short hopelessly unsuited in every way to boarding school life, if not indeed human life generally. Johnny was not entirely innocent – nobody was – of having added to Edwardes' miseries but now, seeing him alone, he felt sorry for him. What was his mother thinking of, buying him sandals like that?

'Well, you know you're not supposed to be here,' said Johnny.

Edwardes did not reply but remained on his knees with his back to Johnny, who suddenly had the feeling that he was weeping as he was wont to do, wetly and silently.

'Come on, Edwardes, it's no good here, you know.' There was something a bit creepy about this altar and crucifix business.

Edwardes got up slowly, crossing himself with a terrific movement of the elbow, and turned round. He was indeed crying, his clothes were more than usually messy and some little stones adhered to his dirty knees. Without any more being said he walked out of the garden, leaving Johnny standing alone before the little altar. It was very depressing.

Johnny returned to his plot in low spirits. How could he help someone like that? He had barely returned to the issue of rows for his peas when little Marvell materialised beside him, regaling ruminatively on a handful of fresh bamboo shoots, a standard dietary supplement at The Dell. In contrast with Edwardes, Marvell was always entirely composed and whereas Edwardes was always at odds with the world Marvell somehow contrived to make the world his friend and get it to minister to him at all points. As already mentioned, he was very small, very young, ginger-haired, freckled and winning in look.

He now merely stood beside Johnny as he worked, watching him.

Although Marvell, like Edwardes, was in the wrong by being there at all Johnny felt scrutinised by this innocent gaze and at a disadvantage. Marvell was the only boy in the school who had once, as if by right, wandered into the staff dining room and sat down in a chair, to the stupefaction of the staff then present; the only boy who had walked down the front stairs – reserved exclusively for staff and the Head Boy – on his first day in the school. He was more like an infant to be indulged or a mascot to be paraded and pampered than an ordinary member of the school. He had the knack of bringing out in people something in them that was usually in abeyance: people were different with him. Johnny was not immune to the pathos that seemed to attend him but he also felt uneasy about the boy.

'What are you doing, Clarke?' piped Marvell.

To one so young the appropriate schoolboy reply of 'What does it look like?' would have been harsh and cynical. Johnny explained what he was doing and they talked. Marvell, it transpired, had a garden at home and indeed a gardener who lived in a little cottage in the grounds. Mr Marvell paid him in pound notes every Saturday morning. Marvell also had a pony, about which he was lengthily informative.

'Isn't that your bell, Marvell?' Johnny enquired, as the first of the evening's tintinnabulations rang out across the grounds.

'Bed time,' said the little boy matter-of-factly and walked off, composed and self-contained, leaving Johnny to wonder whether there wasn't perhaps something about the garden that attracted the oddities – Mr Bolton, Edwardes, Marvell – and –

gosh! – of course, himself. Was he an oddity too? Johnny brought his gardening to an end and went off in search of friends.

The uneasy feeling he had had about the dormitory following the Haines-and-the-curtains episode persisted, though in the days that had followed there had been no animosity between them. Alone that evening as the last and most senior in the bathroom Johnny and Haines now talked as they flapped flannels about and dawdled over brushing their teeth – anything to drag out the time before having to go to bed. The setting sun poured light through the window and a gentleness prevailed.

'I found Edwardes praying this evening,' said Johnny.

'I'm not surprised,' replied Haines, drying his hair vigorously, 'he's crazy, Edwardes.'

'And he's got a terrible temper. I wonder what he'll do in life.'

'Loony bin, I should think,' opined Haines negligently.

'The funny thing is he thinks he's the bees' knees,' said Johnny.

'The cat's pyjamas,' added Haines, and they both fell about laughing. Then suddenly Johnny farted – quite richly.

'Hey – not bad,' said Haines appreciatively and furrowed his brow in an act of concentration, it being the proper response for him to fart too. Generally, if one's companion blew-off one should reciprocate. Not to do so was in effect not only to be uncompanionable but also to have 'lost', whereas to do so promptly and if possible more loudly was both to demonstrate due companionship and also to have 'won'. Haines 'won' on this occasion partly by means of an artificial aid previously undiscovered.

It so happened that at the time of his fundamental expiration Haines was seated on the edge of the bath. Now this bath was fitted with a flat wooden surround designed to enable a number of boys to sit and wash their feet and legs, as they did after games. Wind broken on a hard surface – as of course one knew from class – resonated more satisfactorily than that simply released in the standing position. But there were two other important contributory factors that transformed a fairly modest fart into something in the first league: these were the fact that Haines was naked at the time and that the wooden surface was wet.

'There was a bubble!' shrieked Johnny. 'I swear it – a bubble!'

'Yeah?!' Haines – delighted.

'Gosh, do it again, Haines, go on.'

But Haines, exhilarated by his success and strain though he did, could not. Unlike belching, which even moderate practitioners could perform at will, farting was far less at the command of the subject. Farting was a matter of accident and inspiration, depending on what one had eaten and when last one had had a bowel movement. It was also a matter of natural talent of which some were generously, some not at all, possessed. Haines was at the best of times, though a capable person in many ways, a farter of only moderate calibre.

'Let me have a go.' Johnny whipped down his pyjama bottoms and took up a position on the bench. A moment's waiting was richly rewarded by a detonation that combined a wooden ripping noise with a wet hissing into a fart of hitherto unheard or unimagined quality.

'Crikey!' cried Haines, almost in awe. 'Can you do another one? No, hang on a minute.' And he reached for the soap which, softened by long immersion in the bath, he now applied liberally to the wooden ledge. It did not create a foamy lather but a thick layer of soapy slime which might be expected to deepen and intensify the wet aspect of the fart. 'Now try that.'

Johnny's performance on the prepared patch exceeded his previous number, this one not only resonating and hissing as before, but generating slimy bubbles in gratifying profusion. Johnny and Haines were ecstatic but – alas! – the muse's visitation had run its course in Johnny's system and no more wind would come, strain as he might.

It was with great excitement that they returned to the

dormitory, their sponge-bags whirling about their heads.

'Hey, you lot,' cried Haines on entering, 'Clarke's done some of the most *incredible* – oh! hello, Matron – yes, I'm sorry we're late but we're here now and I'm in bed' – cheekily suiting the action to the word by diving head-first between the sheets and drumming his feet on the pillow.

'Now, calm down,' said Matron, but soon left them to the pleasure of Haines' and Johnny's account of the wondrous soapy farts that had been achieved.

On the strength of his virtuosity in this important area of personal accomplishment Johnny's general popularity and authority were restored and his relationship with Haines became strong and harmonious. To hell with Edwardes.

✳ CHAPTER V ✳

People gifted at sport find ample opportunities for success and achievement; the inept are more likely to experience suffering and persecution. The latter group included Edwardes whose fate took a harsh turn at the swimming pool.

The sporting amenities at The Dell were of the most simple – two rough fields, one of them with a heavy diagonal slope. For such refinements as goal posts with nets behind them or such luxuries as squash courts and shooting ranges boys must await promotion to public school. There was no swimming pool but an arrangement had been made with a local hotel that did possess such an amenity, so that 'swimming' was firmly in the prospectus. It was very popular with the boys, for a variety of reasons, not least the fact that going to the pool meant leaving school premises, a rare treat; also because it made a change from endless cricket, and of course because it was good fun.

There was no instruction involved in swimming; the water of the unheated pool was far too cold to allow of any shivery lingering as instruction was given, even had there been anyone able or inclined to give it. It was just a matter of plunging in, thrashing about and scrambling out again. The pool was not only unheated but uncleaned – indeed untended in any way by the proprietors of the hotel who charged for its use, confident in the knowledge that none of their own guests would ever use it. Arrival at the pool was therefore a moment of some excitement and there was eager competition to get to the pool-side first to inspect and test conditions and report on them to those bringing up the rear of the crocodile. This eagerness was on one occasion richly rewarded by the discovery of a dead rat floating on the surface which Major Oakes was obliged to remove with the shooting-stick with which he was commonly equipped.

The pool contents, having made a clean cold start in early May, changed gradually in temperature and colour as summer advanced, a thin icy blue giving way to a light green which darkened through June so that by the end of term the waters were of a deep Amazonian hue. Thus as the temperature became more inviting the water itself became less so, the bottom even at the shallow end being lost to sight and various small forms of aquatic life developing and going about their business of foraging and procreation.

Even less inviting, at every stage of the season, were the changing rooms. Tucked away into what had once perhaps been a small quarry in scrub below the pool and in deep day-long shade stood a dank and rotting shed sectioned off inside to provide private changing space and a communal urinal. The pungency of the latter was so overpowering and its concrete surrounds so very wet that users stood well clear. In consequence the damp area spread and the pungency increased. In the little cabins damp was triumphant over creosote, and slugs, snails, frogs and other less readily identified creatures took up happy residence. It was with nimble step, as if to avoid putting foot to ground, that the boys escaped from this unappealing place to the sun-filled area of the pool.

Even by those who enjoyed swimming the changing process was regarded with distaste: it was an experience of horror to those who didn't. Most boys enjoy swimming: Edwardes was one of those who didn't. He loathed it. Now it was a principle of school life that no one should ever be 'let off' anything. If you didn't like it – whether the 'it' were rice pudding or swimming – you had to accept it; the rice pudding might be small and the swimming brief but there was no escape. What, after all, might happen if the optional spirit were to take hold? Anybody might refrain from anything they didn't fancy and then where would the world be? Thus the rice-pudding hater must sit over his untasted bowl till four o'clock if necessary and the hydrophobic be dipped in the hated element. It was all 'pour décourager les autres.' So a lot of labour had to go into getting Edwardes through the whole process: he had to be coaxed into the changing cabin, cajoled out again and wheedled – and in the last resort lowered bodily – into the water. He swam a kind of furious doggy-paddle – a desperate fighting with the water – and he kept his head well above the surface so as to protect his face from contact with the dreaded stuff. Simultaneously gasping and groaning through clenched teeth and with painfully screwed up eyes he would make his slow, thrashing progress from one side of the shallow end to the other, this width being sufficient to satisfy the requirement of the master-in-charge. Such was the violence of his response to anyone daring to splash or in any way interfere with his frenzied progress that he was allowed to go his way unmolested. This was all the more remarkable in that, while furiously doggy-paddling, he was at the same time actually walking along the bottom, for he could not swim.

Meanwhile others jumped and raced, crawled and ducked a happy half hour away. Johnny was – although he did his best to conceal it – a reluctant swimmer, having a distrust of water of any depth. He did not like going under and he had never dived. Not that the opportunities for diving other than off the side were good. The springboard had been removed (perhaps because broken) and the high board was so extraordinarily high for a pool of that size that no one was allowed to use it. Some boasted that they would if they were, though probably all felt some secret relief that this boast was secure against proving.

Getting to the hotel from the school was usually an eager

procession, and downhill: returning – by the time they got to the top of the hill, anyway – was a bedraggled rout. It was customary to stop there and regroup for the final quarter-mile or so, to let the stragglers – of whom Edwardes was invariably one – catch up.

But on this particular occasion Edwardes was not among them. It was Johnny who discovered this since he had been instructed by the master-in-charge, Major Oakes, to 'count heads', while he himself gazed vacantly into the distance.

'I think we're one short, sir,' Johnny reported.

'Nonsense – count again.'

Johnny did so. 'We are, sir, and it's Edwardes.'

'Idiot boy!' expostulated Major Oakes, scenting some possible inconvenience for himself. Settling resignedly on his shooting stick, he added, 'He'll be here in a minute.'

But he wasn't.

'Nip back to the hotel, Clarke, and fetch him. I'll go on with this shower. If you're not back at school in fifteen minutes I'll send a search party.'

'May I go with him, sir?' requested Haines, always on the alert for adventure.

'If you must. On the double and don't muck about. You lot – back to school with me.' And he marched away.

Johnny and Haines jogged down the hill, expecting to find Edwardes dawdling along the pavement towards them. But they had not encountered him by the time they reached the hotel.

'Where on earth can he be?' Johnny wondered, pausing at the entrance. 'He wouldn't still be at the pool, would he – the way he hates swimming?'

'He's crazy enough to do anything,' said Haines.

'I say, you don't think he's gone wandering off into the town, do you?'

'The town' was a remote land to boys at The Dell.

'Well, let's check the pool first anyway.'

They ran there. It was a relief to Johnny that Edwardes was

not floating on the surface and the pool water was yet clear enough for them instantly to see that he was not on the bottom either. That seemed to cover the worst eventualities so that now it was merely, in Johnny's mind, a matter of finding the crazy boy. And find him they soon did.

In the furthest and dankest of the little black changing cabins Edwardes was kneeling in his customary attitude of prayer. He had clearly dressed without drying and so looked more of a mess than usual, though of course his ragged mop of hair was dry, at least on top.

'Come on, Edwardes,' said Johnny patiently, 'you've missed the party back.'

To his surprise Edwardes rose, after a moment, to his feet and 'came quietly'. But then he saw Haines, the sheer sight of whom convulsed him into a snorting panic like a goaded bullock and he tore in his ungainly fashion out of the vile shed and back to the pool. The two followed him but were not in time to prevent him climbing the vertical steps up to the high and forbidden diving board. Haines was in the act of following him there when he realised the unwisdom of doing so.

So there stood Johnny and Haines beside the pool below and there above, on – though not at the end of – the high-diving board (the board on which no boy from The Dell had ever set foot let alone from which he had ever dived), stood Edwardes.

'Now what are you going to do, Edwardes, you loony?' shouted Haines.

'Clear off , Haines,' retorted Edwardes, not looking down and standing rigidly on high. The impetuous force which had driven him, probably without due premeditation, up the diving board had now run into a sudden cul-de-sac and stopped dead. On arriving at the top he froze, as non-plussed by his situation as were his would-be rescuers. None there knew what to do.

'Be ready if he jumps,' whispered Johnny to Haines. 'Remember – he can't swim.'

Haines grunted in acknowledgement.

'Come on, Edwardes,' Johnny attempted with an assumed casualness, 'we'll miss lunch at this rate. Do you want me to come up and help you down?'

In fact Edwardes did, but having adopted a position of such flagrant defiance his proud soul could not now instantly capitulate. His first setting foot on the bottom rung of the ladder – a small, as it seemed to him, gesture of escape – had now committed him quite beyond his powers to a complete ascent and the assumption of an impossibly precarious position.

'Don't be a heathen, Edwardes,' called Haines in less sympathetic tones, deliberately employing Edwardes' single and powerful term of abuse.

'Shut up, Haines!' cried Edwardes, through clenched teeth, instantly enraged.

'You're a flipping heathen, Edwardes,' persisted Haines. 'Aren't you?'

Johnny intervened. 'What are you doing, Haines?' he hissed, his eye nervously fixed on the figure on high who was now both rigid with vertigo and quivering with rage : ordinarily on dry land Edwardes would have been roaring and flailing his fists at such provocation.

'I'm deliberately trying to make him angry,' Haines whispered in reply. 'If he gets in a rage he'll come down to try and beat me up.'

In the circumstances – i.e., bleak – Johnny thought this a brilliant idea. Edwardes was clearly not going to respond to blandishment or cajolery but anger might well be the emotion to move his passionate soul to constructive action.

'A bloody heathen,' called up Haines in furtherance of his tactic.

'Shut up, shut up!' shrieked Edwardes. 'Don't swear.'

Haines piled on the agony. 'You're a bloody hairy heathen, I say.'

Edwardes' fists and arms could be seen to convulse with energy restrained and a low, strangled gargling was heard. The twitchings of his body suggested that he wanted to turn round through the half circle required (facing towards the dreaded pool) and descend but diving boards do not admit of such a manoeuvre except by a person possessed of a control and assurance quite outside Edwardes' capability at the calmest of times. To get down he was going to have to do so backwards.

Unperceiving of this predicament, Haines delivered the coup de grace. 'You're not only a bloody heathen, Edwardes – you're a bloody atheist.'

On this terrible word the irresistible force could be resisted no more. With an enraged roar Edwardes released the pent-up energy of body and soul and swung into that act of tergiversation required for a descent of the diving board rungs preparatory to a merciless lambasting of the blasphemous Haines with his righteous fists. Alas – as has been pointed out – the narrowness of the board did not admit of such a manoeuvre and Edwardes teetered, toppled and plunged.

The piercing yell he emitted – a cry of rage, compounded with fear of heights, the deep and simple terror of falling and the loathing of water – was swiftly shut off as his flailing, and of course fully-clothed, body met the water, back first, with a smacking splash that showered the two rescuers riveted to the pool-side with fascination and fear.

The anxiety, intensified in Johnny's heart during the short seconds of falling, that Edwardes would require life-saving at Haines' – not his own – hands, was replaced by the fear that he was going to hit the side of the pool, to die rather by concussion than by drowning, for in falling the direction of Edwardes' intended turn threw him more towards that murderous concrete edge than out into the relatively safe waters of the pool. However, he just missed, and it was no great difficulty for the two boys to manhandle the dripping wretch out of the pool and into an inert but living bundle on the safety of the pool-side. With a great deal of sputtering and spitting Edwardes was dragged to his feet by helping hands and, the picture of a spirit doused, was escorted back to school in a silence broken only by the repetitious squelching of pool water from his extraordinary sandals.

To acclamation. Their entry into the building took them past the window of the dining room in which the entire school was now at meat. On the terrace, before the French windows, they passed and, while every boy clambered for a view behind him – 'It's Edwardes, he's soaking!' – Mr Victor emerged to confront the trio: the two rescuers, weary but proud of their suddenly dramatic role, and the yet dripping Edwardes, slumped between them, his curly hair flattened to his head, his grey uniform dark with damp, water oozing away at his feet, his holy zeal quenched. The Headmaster was lost for words.

CHAPTER VI

Of such challenges did the Head of School's role appear to be composed. But a break from this responsibility and indeed, more excitingly, from school life soon appeared when Johnny was called upon to sit the Worthington scholarship exam.

Whereas the ordinary lucky characters who would be sitting the Common Entrance exam did so in the reassuringly familiar context of The Dell, scholarship candidates were required to undergo the trials of examination at the public school whose academic gauntlet they were courageously taking up. To Worthington therefore one bright day in May Johnny was driven in the worthy Vauxhall by his father.

For little of this experience did he feel prepared. He had never visited the school, as neither had his father. He had been entered for the scholarship because the school offered a substantial bursary for the son of a clergyman who evinced sufficient academic promise to warrant it, it being often the case that the children of a clergyman were as clever as he was impecunious. This was Mr Victor's idea.

Worthington, healthily situated on a spur of the South Downs not far from a popular sea-side resort on the south coast, had been founded in early Victorian times before the days of universal schooling by a young clergyman of passionate educational, social and moral convictions, inspired by the Tractarian movement to re-evangelise the burgeoning middle-class. These convictions and aspirations were all powerfully symbolised in the construction of an enormous school chapel which, lofty and prominent, commanded a fine view of the suburban littoral and the sea beyond. It was a famed landmark for miles.

And indeed the whole school was built on a scale that was quite beyond Johnny's experience and he felt initially overpowered by the towers and spires – these were actually singular but struck him in their awesomeness as plural – the quadrangles, the cloisters, steps and gateways that the school was composed of. He did not, on first arriving at this impressive place, see how anything he had or knew could possibly qualify him for membership of – let alone academically honourable status in – such an august establishment.

He was also discouraged, after having been duly delivered into appropriate hands by his father, by the dozen or so other prep school boys – one of them a black boy – who like himself had come to attempt an academic assault upon this seemingly impregnable fortress of learning. If they were not the obvious 'brain-box' type with intent looks on their pale and bespectacled faces, they all seemed, in their wearing of colourful blazers richly braided and badged, to have automatic superiority over him whose suit – he did not possess a blazer – grey, second-hand and not quite matching as to its two parts, seemed irretrievably dowdy. Several of them came from the same school and some had obviously encountered on fields of play on their local sporting circuit from which The Dell was remote. In short, Johnny was paralysed by a feeling of total academic and social inferiority.

Over the period of the examination – about three or four days – the candidates were accommodated in the sanatorium, a low building set amongst wind-bent sycamores on the seaward extremity of the school grounds. Though not exactly homely, being presided over by a uniformed sister permanently garbed for medical action and hung about with small instruments – her fierce mien put her in an unpleasing contrast with the ample blue bosominess of 'Matron' at The Dell – the sanatorium had none of that daunting stateliness of the remainder of the school and Johnny was at least relieved of the fear that he would have to sleep in a dormitory whose inmates might be inclined to visit unpleasantnesses on a naïve interloper, as he had understood was the practice in public schools. Here the candidates slept – though they ate in the Dining Hall at a small separate table – and did their papers, as if scholarship candidacy were an affliction that, though giving no cause for alarm, required firm isolation.

And the examination procedure itself was daunting. For one thing the papers were all properly printed like pamphlets unlike any other exam papers he had ever sat, all of which – including the famously bamboozling Winchester scholarship questions with which Mr Victor delighted to confound his star pupils – were hand-written by their setters and rolled off on a machine whose temperamental character put Mr Denman into constant frenzies and whose products smelled more powerfully than they could be easily deciphered.

Invigilation was by a master wearing a gown, a garment hitherto unknown to Johnny, the possession of which suggested to him the existence of levels of academic achievement quite beyond his powers.

The exam papers followed one another in quick succession so that the depressing experience of one was quickly displaced by the depressing experience of the next. In the first Latin paper Johnny found himself working uphill through a passage of unseen prose wrought by a minor Roman historian whose style combined syntactical density with obscurity of vocabulary in a puzzling manner. Having eventually wriggled his way through this thicket, Johnny found himself short of time for the grammar question and the concluding prose, during which he felt his command of tenses slip away from him.

The first Maths paper was no more difficult than those to which he was accustomed and he completed it as best he could:

like a one-handed batsman, aware of his fundamental disability, but willing to do his duty by staying at the crease as long as he could and perhaps edging a lucky single or two. The second Maths paper, however, proved completely bewildering, containing some Greek symbols he had simply never encountered in a mathematical context before, so that while the other candidates seemed happily wrapped in a productive cerebration aided by metal and plastic instruments of which he was not possessed, Johnny spun out for as long as he could his calculations over the single question (of ten) that seemed to afford him any sort of intellectual handhold. By the end of the exam his efforts – including deletions – barely covered a side while other candidates handed in several sheets.

As if this had not been enough to depress his spirits Johnny soon found himself confronted by the Science paper. Now he had been given by Mr Victor to understand that because of the small amount of instruction he had received in it he would not be required to sit that particular subject. He did not, however, when it was put before him, have the courage to remonstrate with the gowned invigilator and was thus condemned to another unproductive hour and a half. Whereas the nation's famous war leader had, when similarly challenged in his youth, managed no more than the simple inscription of his name, duly, upon reflection, underlined, Johnny eventually, having rejected the idea of volunteering his version of the composition of the atom, summoned the courage to write a sentence to the effect that he was unable to do this paper since he knew no Science. This sentence, after a Churchillian period of reflection, he put in brackets and, with blushes, handed in his paper to an impassive invigilator.

It was not until the General Paper that Johnny felt at all sure of his ground, for essay-writing was his strength. He now wrote with some confidence and in considerable detail on the topic 'Town versus Country'. For years he had been trained by Mr Victor in the skills of taking some simple term or topic – as, for example, not long before, 'Harvest' – and, dividing it into constituent parts, treating them sequentially and framing them with an introductory and a concluding paragraph. Thus, in his plan for 'Harvest' he had had:

1. Introductory: the blessings of harvest; bread etc.
2. a) Ploughing.
   b) Sowing.
   c) Growing.
   d) Reaping.
3. Men and machinery; the old and the new.
4. Sunshine and shower; poppies and larks.
5. Concluding: Harvest Festival.

When it came to the English paper, however, Johnny passed over a further opportunity to exercise his skill in this kind of essay work that had been such an ornament of English letters for hundreds of years – 'A Seaside Holiday', for example, seemed to have some quite promising possibilities like the movements of the tide, sandcastles, rock-pools, donkey-rides etc. – and instead plumped for a title that prompted something more fictional or at any rate imaginative: The Brink.

He wrote – no doubt unconsciously inspired by the memory of Edwardes' recent adventure – about a man who positioned himself to commit suicide by hurtling from a high diving board into an empty swimming pool. A sufficiently dramatic resolution to this fiction proved elusive to its author but Johnny finally settled on a grand moment in which helicopters, coming upon the scene without warning and in some numbers, dropped huge balloons of water into the pool in quick succession, thereby depriving the would-be suicide of the lethally concussive property of the concrete bottom. The want of verisimilitude in this denouement troubled him little as his pen sped eagerly on. Story-writing did not come into Mr Victor's notion of English. Writing stories was for the young and indeed Johnny had in his earlier years in the school proved successful in that field, as witness the fact that Mrs Logsdon of

Form 1 had kept some of his pencilled fictions for reading to ensuing years as an inspiration to their own fictional efforts.

Telling stories in the dormitory after lights-out as a popular diversion was one of Johnny's social recommendations but his creations in that context were too whimsical or scurrilous to have any connection with a proper written narrative such as – after several years' lack of practice – he now wrote.

'Where are we going next?' he found himself asking the black boy whose name, though Johnny had heard it – it was long, rich in vowels and impossible to remember – he did not now therefore use. They were walking in the self-conscious gaggle which had almost begun to give the scholarship candidates some kind of identity in the place after a swim in the pool which had been not only indoor but both warm and clean – the black boy had not participated – towards one of the school's numerous large buildings.

'Music' was the laconic reply. Johnny had tried to befriend this boy, partly out of fascination with his colour – he had never seen a black person at close quarters before – and partly identifying him, like himself, as an odd one out in the group. But he was not a willing conversationalist. Duly arrived at the music school they were met by a stereotypically maned music master who thrust musical instruments indiscriminately into their hands and required each to perform upon whatever he held. Johnny found himself clasping a trumpet, from which, when his time came – he had been given some perfunctory practical introduction – he could not produce anything better than a strangulated gasp. Music was another of those spheres of education – why did there have to be so many? – in which Johnny was incapable. At The Dell it did exist as a subject but only in the form of class singing, though one or two boys were instructed in the piano by a woman who appeared twice-weekly and taught on the battered instrument on which Mr Blackstone was wont to extemporise by way of general entertainment. So the boys could all sing *The British Grenadiers* and *Hearts of Oak* but they were otherwise musically unlearned. There was a sort of band that performed in end-of-term concerts but its instrumentation was limited to the lavatory-paper-on-a-comb device which created a noise like bees humming melodiously inside a small lampshade.

Johnny, defeated by the trumpet, thought of volunteering to sing instead but refrained. His dark-skinned companion absolutely refused to attempt anything on the oboe that he reluctantly held or, when an alternative was offered, anything else. The music master, defeated, muttered something racially offensive about drums but that was the end of it. Johnny was much impressed by the boy's unshakeable stolidity as a form of protest though he could not begin to imagine adopting such a stance himself.

The most challenging experience of them all was his interview with the headmaster, not least because he had no idea of the nature and function of such a test. Dr Woolf blended oily charm, enthusiasm and learning with immense height to an over-powering degree and his study – of which there appeared to Johnny to be about half an acre – was, in contrast with Mr Victor's pitiful garret, so rich in objects of a silver, china, wooden and pictorial variety that Johnny was inescapably distracted from the questions that Dr Woolf was genially but relentlessly plying him with. The question 'With what words does the Nicene Creed open?' – a special one perhaps for the sons-of-clergy applicants – was not easy to answer when he was trying to make sense of a bronze on the mantelpiece which appeared, at a distance, to represent two figures – one human (or perhaps animal), one animal (or perhaps human) – who were interlocked in an inexplicable manner.

With this crowning experience of humiliation at Worthington Johnny returned again by means of parental Vauxhall to The Dell. He was not sure how the Worthington response to his efforts would be communicated to him but he was preparing to watch Mr Victor's post pretty closely over the next few days. He was in a position to do so, since as Head of School he had the privilege of sitting on the headmaster's right hand in the dining room. On the headmaster's breakfast side-plate the post was laid so that during porridge he would leaf through its contents and examine postmarks, during egg he would open and read selected items, and during bread and marmalade he would tear off the stamps and pass them to the second head of school, Balmforth, on his left. The post, the morning after Johnny's return, contained an unusual item – a telegram. Johnny did not think to associate so urgent and expensive a communication with himself but he was not surprised to see Mr Victor's attention caught by it at an early stage of the riffling process and his knife slit it open. On perusal Mr Victor blinked and stared, then tapped the handle-end of his knife on the table at which familiar signal the school, never rowdy at breakfast, fell instantly silent. And then, holding the telegram aloft like a statesman in triumph, he announced 'You will all be glad to know that Clarke has won a Clergy Exhibition to Worthington.' Sitting down amidst spontaneous cheers he leaned towards Johnny to say 'Well done,' small particles of porridge exploding from his lips with this unprecedented felicitation.

❊ CHAPTER VII ❊

By the time he went to bed that night he had had one of the best days school had ever afforded him. Johnny did not expect much from school, which was just as well since it rarely offered much, but sometimes – without warning – it could shower gold. For not only did the day begin with the wonderful news of his Exhibition – he had not for a moment considered that he had a chance of success – but it was also, coincidentally, the day of the Choir Outing.

Summer terms were usually dominated by events and occasions, mainly of course by the crucial harvesting at Common Entrance of the academic grain so long and carefully nurtured through the seasons, but in other ways also, of which, at The Dell, the two most important were Sports Day and The Play. Of these two more will be heard later, for the present concern is with the Choir Outing. This had been instituted in the mists of the school's early history when a successful river excursion one year had been repeated the next to find itself in year three, and thereafter, firmly entrenched as an immutable tradition. Although it involved no more than fifteen boys or so it was jealously treasured by the lucky participants and touched on in conversation throughout the year. Legend had grown up around it that deepened that anticipation, legends the details of which were relished in the company of Mrs Victor when she was on matron duty and in a good mood, conditions that did occasionally coincide. Mrs Victor was inclined to play down the more dramatic elements and colourful embellishments to these legends when boys sought to draw from her at least a confirmation if not, as they hoped, an elaboration of a particular historical incident. 'Well, very nearly...' she might say in response to the eager allegation that one year Mr Victor had become separated from his punt pole and fallen into the river; or 'We were afraid that might happen but it didn't actually...' when asked to recount the famous occasion when Mr Blackstone's skiff had gone over the weir with all hands. But Mrs Victor's little reservations in the interests of veracity (for whose smallest details she had the deepest respect) laid no constraint on the imaginations that embellished and distorted it in the hungry interests of wonder and excitement. Mr Victor, it might be asserted one summer's evening after 'lights-out', *had* one year been left clinging to the top of the pole as the punt, full of boys and sandwiches drifted away from him inexorably; Jenkins *had*, only two years previously, slipped over in a cow-pat during the famous game of rounders and it certainly *had* happened one year that it had rained so hard that boating was out of the question – the famous picnic had been eaten in the shelter of the village hall in an atmosphere of some gloom until someone had had the wildly improbable idea of going for a night-time swim in the pouring rain at the hotel pool and it had turned out to be one of the best Choir Outings ever. The celebration of these legends might be extended and enriched by debate over details – it was a boy called Aspinall, not Jenkins, who had gone a purler into the cow-pat, for example – and also by a few whose respect for truth approached Mrs Victor's and whose intervention served to sharpen the edge of debate and occasionally to intensify it to the point of argument.

A sunny day became a sunny evening and that half of the choir not chosen to travel in the convenience of the Victors' car which bore, in addition to its owners, the all-important picnic and the more junior members, like Marvell, who should be spared, in deference to their tender years, the demands of the long walk to the boat station – that sturdy band then made their cheerful way to the point of embarkation. There Mr Victor, as usual leaving things to the last moment, was in negotiation with the proprietor of the boatyard over the matter of which craft were to be hired. A difficulty had arisen over the punt which, since Mr Victor had not specifically booked it, the man explained, and since, it not being a popular choice in the general way, it had not been used so far that season, was therefore not in full readiness. In fact, though it was in the water rather than in some dank corner of the yard, it sat under an alder tree a little way down the bank, rather too full of rainwater and detached vegetation for immediate use let alone comfort, looking well set for an irreversible decline into a watery grave. Might Mr Victor not be happy to take another skiff instead, suggested the proprietor anxiously – a fine new one had been added to the fleet that year? This suggestion received not the scantest consideration: to the entire party, not Mr Victor alone, the idea that the headmasterly punt should be exchanged for a mere rowing boat was out of the question: the quintessential character of the expedition would be unacceptably degraded. No, no – the punt must be made ready whatever its present condition. Instantly all hands turned to this crucial task. The boatyard's one baler was augmented by a dustpan and some tin cups for the rapid emptying of the rainwater; leaves and twigs were picked and flicked away by willing fingers; the old brown corduroy-covered cushions were unearthed from the back of the boatshed, dusted down with hearty whacks and – the boat now cleaned out and standing rather more proud in the water – set in their proper places on its bottom and against its adjustably-reclining seat-backs.

Not without misgivings did the venerable boat's proprietor – who had intended last September to replace the metal ferrule of the punt's pole but never got round to doing so – watch these proceedings, followed as they were by the punt's water-line sinking once more under the burden of picnic and people and by its eventual casting off, the last of three craft in the flotilla, the other two being a skiff and a canoe. The latter, built in imitation of that designed by Red Indians, with high curling prow and stern, was requisitioned by the more adventurous souls who took their places and their paddles with eager confidence to be the first to shoot away from the jetty and scout on ahead with determined speed, adventuring close to banks and up little side-waters, while the former, officially captained by Mr Blackstone, zig-zagged uncertainly behind. Mr Blackstone interpreted his captaincy in a rather passive manner, lounging Cleopatra-like in the stern of the boat while small boys crawled dangerously about him and inexperienced oarsmen lunged and struck errantly. The headmasterly punt brought up the rear in a stately manner, Mr Victor himself, positioned on the raised end of the craft in the Cambridge manner, from which he propelled the boat at a regular pace and in an unswerving direction. For this expedition he wore white flannels and a boater in the fashion of an age now passing and frayed as to blazer and cravat that completed the outfit. Such was the dexterity of his punting that not a drop of water splashed from pole to costume. At his feet huddled Mrs Victor, at her own feet the picnic stored in a wicker laundry basket, and such boys, including Johnny, as had been unsuccessful in securing places in one of the other craft not containing Mr Victor.

Uneventful was the progress upriver to the invariable picnic place. The river itself was narrow, dark, slow-moving, in parts almost like a canal. Under trees and bridges, between weed-fringed banks they passed, the westering sun softening the evening light and showing up clouds of insects dancing above the water.

'What's The Play going to be this year, sir?' asked Johnny.

Mr Victor, expansive in mood, had been animadverting to the beauties of the scene and had even been drawn, while they were in the preparatory stages of launching, into quoting the lines 'There is nothing half so much worth doing as simply messing about in boats.' Johnny thought he might be disposed to talk on that one subject the discussion of which immediately put a fresh and positive glint in Mr Victor's eye.

The Play, as it was simply known, was the climax and the conclusion of the summer term and the school year. It was produced by Mr Victor with the assistance – in some cases voluntary, in others not – of many boys and all members of staff, particularly of Mr Blackstone, who not only stood in for Mr Victor in the numerous rehearsals that the headmaster was too busy to take but also directed the music (if there were any) and designed and painted the set (such as it was) that Mr Denman built.

Mr Victor was in fact in a position to give Johnny an answer to his question but he did not do so. Normally he did not choose his play – some straightforward drama suitable for the young (though in truth such were few) – until a couple of months before performance but he had this year, in collaboration with Mr Blackstone, made a plan which was yet to be declared: they were to do a Gilbert and Sullivan operetta.

Simple ambition was one motive for this new venture. It would go down well with the parents who would see their son's school breaking new cultural ground in its upward movement to the ranks of the more prestigious prep schools. Another was the opportunity – tempting but not taken in previous years – to play a part himself. This had always been an ambition of his since his frequent participation in college productions at Cambridge but he had not indulged it, contenting himself with direction and showing the boys 'how it was to be done'. Gilbert and Sullivan offered numerous baritone lead parts that would be well beyond the capability of a thirteen-year-old but well within his own. *The Mikado* was his choice and therefore Ko Ko his part. He had already mastered many of the lines and, in private, was now in the habit of quietly singing them over to himself. He had considerable reservations about the abilities of the boys to fill the other singing roles – little did poor Johnny know that he was already in Mr Victor's mind (for want of anyone better rather than for his suitability for the part) marked down as the 'thing of shreds and patches', but he and Mr Blackstone would overcome all obstacles, Mr Blackstone fired by this new musical challenge.

So, although not yet ready to let the cat out of the bag, Mr Victor could not resist dropping some hint and therefore replied 'Perhaps something a little different this year.'

'Perhaps something musical, sir?' queried another boy with an accuracy entirely fortuitous.

'Perhaps,' replied Mr Victor with finality and a smile.

The choir picnic was always taken in a riverside meadow rich in gnats and buttercups. A feast of Heinz Sandwich Spread sandwiches and Mrs Bolton's cold bread pudding washed down with orange squash diluted to the point of tastelessness was followed by the traditional game of rounders in which all joined.

In theory rounders was a despised game fit only for infants and girls; in practice, since it was pleasantly free of anxieties about bowling to a length and playing the proper stroke that cast such a pall of seriousness upon the cricket field, it was hugely popular on this occasion. Instead of bowling one simply hurled the thing; instead of playing a straight bat one simply took a mighty swipe. It was deeply satisfying also, having taken one's swipe, then to hurl the stick far away as one tore off to first base. Even timid Mrs Victor posed the stick to the ball and was wildly cheered around the circle while fielders fumbled; even Mr Blackstone ran – an extraordinary and comical sight; even Marvell, specially provided with a less weighty stick and given a 'dolly' to hit, had some success. Great and joyous was the cheering and jeering of the fielding onlookers, high were the cries of the triumphant and deep the groans of the defeated as all took their turn at the 'crease' and, tearing round the circle, made their way panting back to their team.

Eventually, the shadows lengthening across the field, the choir, subdued by their exertion, returned to the boats for the journey home. Traditionally then they sang, Mr and Mrs Victor giving the lead from behind with a familiar selection of songs sacred and secular. Somehow all the irregularities and difficulties of paddling and rowing evened out as the three boats moved gently through the calm waters, propelled as it were by song. The twenty-third Psalm, adopted by the school as its own special one, always featured centrally in this collection and when 'the table was spread' before them they all knew that they had even now enjoyed such a feast while the 'waters of comfort' were there beneath them, buoying them gently along; and if the over-arching alders and willows at times suggested 'the valley of the shadow of death' then this contentment bulwarked them against the fear of evil. How should such an evening end but with quiet joy? How did such an evening end but in unforeseen disaster?

Mr Victor, perhaps seduced into a fatal inadvertence by his melodious adoration of the daughter of Shenandoah, had upthrust his pole into an unusually thick branch above, which, twining itself about the pole as the punt moved on beneath, rendered the removal of the pole impossible. Johnny, facing, saw it well, and whereas another in his position might have hoped to witness the comic spectacle of legend – Mr Victor clinging to a pole separated from its punt – he felt panic suddenly seize at his heart, felt all his insecurity about deep water rush into his soul. Unknowingly he had at the outset allowed himself to choose to be in Mr Victor's boat because the strength of the man and the sturdy construction of the craft promised most safety; now suddenly, song dying on his lips, he was to lose his protection, while the boat, abandoning its captain, was to drift inexorably over the weir where they would all be drowned in the swirling brown waters. But so terrible a fantasy was not actually to be realised. Mr Victor, determined not to be reduced to the danger and indignity of legendary pole-clinging, gave a sudden violent wrench that, tearing the pole free from its detaining branch as intended, shot him forward so that he stumbled, one foot going off the edge of the platform on which he stood and on to the bottom proper of the punt. The force of the foot, Mr Victor being not a light man, was too much for the construction of the boat which, weakened with age, neglect and rot, cracked audibly. It is tempting to say – and future legend might well recount it so – that Mr Victor's foot 'went through it'. It did not, but effectively caused a rift between bottom and side that instantly resulted in a considerable and unstoppable inrush of water.

One of the problems with almost any disaster in its early stages is that nobody involved knows, or correctly gauges, quite what is happening. Mr Victor was preoccupied with recovering his equilibrium, his punt pole and his dignity and therefore did not notice what he had done, while his passengers were screened from view of the fatal leak by the back of the seat on which Mrs Victor was sitting. It was in fact she who raised the alarm as, perceiving bilge waters to be spreading unreasonably fast about her legs, she located the problem. Water was rolling up in the side of the punt very rapidly in the manner of a spring and Mr Victor, once he had seen it, instantly realised the severity of the situation.

'Stay up forrard!' he ordered peremptorily – his command of nautical jargon not deserting him at this moment of crisis – as his passengers naturally got to their feet in anxiety and moved down the boat to see the incoming water. Mrs Victor had also risen in order to avoid getting soaked, the floor cushions were beginning to float and the punt had an appreciable list on its holed side and the bow was beginning to lift.

'Sit down,' now commanded Mr Victor, still not sure what to do but at least confident from experience that an angry shout would relieve his feelings and perhaps point the way to effective action. The action he did take – realising the paramount importance of getting the punt as close as possible to what he hoped to be shallow water near the bank – was to plunge his trusty pole in and give one mighty shove in order to propel them all to safety before the punt – as he was aware it very soon would do wherever they were – sank beneath them. It was a mighty thrust indeed and while it did have the propulsive effect intended it also accelerated the downward plunge of the stern, the platform on which Mr Victor stood becoming submerged and the water pouring into the body of the boat from that direction as well as from the original crack, itself now much enlarged by the inrush of water and its accumulating weight together with the misguided stumblings about of the panic-stricken passengers.

Within moments and still almost in mid-stream the punt sank. Mr Victor, on the stern, was the first to go, slipping clumsily rather than tumbling comically into the murky water. Others, of which Johnny was one, simply took to the water as swimmers as it rose around them. Suppressing panic, Johnny swam the few strokes necessary to reach the bank and there heaved himself to safety. It was not until he was once on dry land that he gave a thought to his fellow passengers. These, however, were all – Mr Victor helping Mrs Victor – now nearly as safe as he and he realised that in fact the punt had sunk in little more than three feet of water. To walk ashore would have been possible.

The occupants of the other boats had of course by now noted and responded to their fellow craft's distress, too late, however, to effect any human rescue – not that that was, fortunately, necessary – but not too late to save the laundry basket and the seat cushions from loss. The three intrepids in the canoe paddled gleefully in pursuit of Mr Victor's boater that threatened to disappear downstream like Ophelia's crownet of weeds, and the situation was saved.

Uncertain as to how the survivors of the punt would be responding to this traumatic experience the others gathered round solicitously with nothing to offer but sympathy should that commodity be called for. As they all, mostly in silence, watched the last bubbles rise from the sunken punt Mr Blackstone said 'There is nothing – absolutely nothing – half so worthwhile doing…' and they all burst into laughter. It was the stuff of legends.

❊ CHAPTER VIII ❊

A few days later Mr Victor heard in more detail from Worthington about Johnny's performance in the scholarship exam. Whereas Dr Woolf's telegram had been thrilling his letter was depressing, and that day had also in store an event that was as miserable as the Choir Outing had been enjoyable.

The letter was quite lengthy – Johnny was privileged to read it in the honourable discomfort of the arm-chair with the leather-strap ash-tray in Mr Victor's study after breakfast – and ranged over the whole of Johnny's performance. His General Paper question had been well argued and he had interviewed quite soundly. That his English, with its powerful and imaginative story and correctly answered grammar questions, had been much his best paper came as no surprise to him.

It was most prominently on the strength of this that Johnny had been judged eligible for the award of the Worthington Clergy Exhibition. This was not great in monetary terms, Mr Victor now explained, but quite definitely an honour and one to be added to Macpherson's Marlborough scholarship on the school honours board. Mr Victor was distinctly pleased, as was his father whom Johnny had been permitted – much to his embarrassment – to telephone himself with the news from Mr Victor's study and in his presence on the day of the telegram.

It was not, however, only Johnny's English that drew

commendation from Dr Woolf: his Latin also, it appeared, was above the common run (though for his Greek, which Johnny had only studied in a few of Mr Victor's free moments over a short period, there could be little praise). And in praise of his performance in other subjects Dr Woolf was notably sparing. The opening of a new paragraph in the letter and the deepening of the tone struck by a ponderous 'However...' was a dire augury of what was to come. Johnny's performance in the first Maths paper was as lamentable as he had supposed and for his work in the second paper the examiner had found it impossible to award him a single mark: in the first Johnny had scraped together the meagre total of 8% – substantially, Dr Woolf felt compelled to say, below the standard required of even a commoner entrant. This total want of mathematical understanding must be remedied before Johnny came to Worthington. Dr Woolf's statement, in fine, of Johnny's situation was this: he was young – only just thirteen – he had barely begun Greek in which other members of the Classics Remove – the form in which he would be entering the school – would be much more advanced; he was also an innocent in Science. In view of these factors it seemed to Dr Woolf sensible for Johnny to remain at The Dell for another two terms instead of coming on the following September. The clergy bursary, of course, would be his when he arrived and he would join the Classics Remove with a stronger base than he appeared at present to have, though there must be the possibility of his remaining in that form for a further full year if necessary. It would be to his advantage in the long run.

This was grave news to Johnny but it was not in his character or upbringing to think of contesting it and he took it with all the weight of an adamantine judgment. Johnny's father wrestled feebly with Mr Victor over it when he detected Johnny's lack of enthusiasm but he was quickly persuaded by Mr Victor who accepted it himself for at least two reasons: one, the simply financial, that it would keep a fee-paying member of the school on the books for a further two terms; another that he was not wholly dissatisfied with Johnny's performance as Head of School, knowing from experience how very few boys there were nowadays who seemed to have any leadership qualities – God knew there were none in the offing – and how tiring it was to train them in the role for they had no sooner achieved some competence in it than they left the school.

Johnny's heart groaned: two more terms, and he realised now how much his spirit had depended on leaving The Dell at the end of this one. It would be intolerable to remain there when his friends and contemporaries had left, not only with the arduous and sometimes bitter task of leading the school but also – and here Johnny's imagination ran off into all sorts of situations where his natural boyishness would be in conflict with the demands of Mr Victor. These images of protracted durance were leaden weights on his soul so that his lonely work that evening in the kitchen garden seemed like the first stretch of a long period of penal servitude – not only the whole of the rest of the term in prospect, but the following football term with its long dark evenings and then through Christmas to the Easter Term with its 'flu and frozen hockey pitches. In such a heart-sick mood, scratching disconsolately at his soil like a prisoner of war in a concentration camp, Johnny had no welcome for the diminutive, ginger-haired figure of Marvell. He had no patience and goodwill with which to meet the naïve retailing of characters and experiences at home, separation from which was clearly a source of deep and continuous distress to the little boy though he hardly knew it himself. But it was not with such that Marvell now, taking up his customary stance, entertained his captive audience. Without preamble he simply said 'Mr Blackstone's been fiddling me' – just like that.

Johnny continued his work, head bent. There could be no question of what Marvell had said nor of what he meant. 'Fiddling' was the common term for a not uncommon practice. It meant playing with the cock of another boy. While not uncommon the practice was not universal nor consistently indulged in. There were one or two boys who did it more often than others, there were periods in a dorm's life when it was quite general. It was commonest, however, when boys from one dorm joined those in another to hear Mr Victor read before lights out.

Mr Victor, harassed and overworked though he was, gave a great amount of time to the reading of stories to older boys. Though the school library still contained volumes of an outdated sort written with the proper education of the sons of Empire in mind in which young Englishmen, often barely more than boys, engaged in deeds of derring-do, such were not Mr Victor's choice for reading aloud but rather an eclectic mixture of the 'classic' children's books and middle-brow authors now almost forgotten, like W.W. Jacobs, A.E.W. Mason – *The Four Feathers* he never tired of – Charles Morgan, Neville Shute – *The Pied Piper* was a favourite – and John Buchan as well as *Treasure Island* and *Ivanhoe*. All these – while not of the old imperial tub-thumping sort – nonetheless implicitly promoted wholesome adventure. On these reading occasions boys from a visiting dormitory shared beds with the hosts. This of course gave ample opportunity for 'fiddling'. Little did Mr Victor know and bitter would his heart have been had he done so how much sexual activity proceeded under the bedclothes while he read, how many sexual careers were launched within sound of his voice. In Johnny's case a strongly restraining hand reached down from the Rectory but even so he did not regard 'fiddling' as a crime.

But this was different. Fiddling between boys was one thing. Fiddling involving a member of staff Johnny, although he had never reflected on it, instinctively and instantly recognised was another. He realised also – not that he could have explained why – that Mr Blackstone was the fiddling type.

What, however, should he do? Marvell had thus far not elaborated on his bald statement which had perhaps been quite difficult for him to make or indeed proceeded in any other conversational direction. He appeared to be just waiting.

'You say he fiddled you?' Johnny queried lamely.

'Yes,' was the reply.

'Oh.' Another pause. He couldn't leave it at that. 'When? Where?'

'Yesterday, on the Choir Outing.'

'You mean, in front of everybody?'

'No, under the rug, in the boat.'

'I see.' Further pause. 'Have you told anyone else?' Naturally Johnny hoped so.

'No.'

'Oh'

Johnny was then revolving some temporizing phrase like 'You'd better keep away from him in future' when Marvell, hearing his dormitory bell, said goodbye and walked off in his composed and slightly mincing step.

What should he do? The problem was laid fairly and squarely by Marvell at his, Johnny's door, and no one else's. His heart sank yet further. It was a very serious matter. It was deeply wrong of Mr Blackstone to fiddle Marvell and there would be dire consequences. But could he, Johnny, be responsible for putting those dire consequences in train? Could he, as it were, sneak on a master? Perhaps he could have a word with Dad at the next exeat, perhaps talk it over with Haines, perhaps with Balmforth, the deputy Head of School with whom he had no fellow-feeling whatever. Or perhaps it was something he ought to be able to handle himself – after all, he was Head of School. Perhaps he should go to Mr Blackstone and confront him with what Marvell had said. No, that was unthinkable.

Clearly there was nothing he could do about it himself directly: he must tell Mr Victor. Hadn't his headmaster enjoined him in his beginning-of-term pep-talk to keep him in touch with what was going on? Here was something 'going on' all right. So he would tell Mr Victor – that was the thing to do.

That decision gave some relief. There was no feeling of relief in his heart, however, the following morning as he stood outside Mr Victor's study after breakfast. Had Marvell actually been telling the truth? Did he in his innocence know what fiddling really was? Perhaps Mr Blackstone had done something much less serious – stroked his hair, or something and Marvell, having got hold of a big boys' word had used it incorrectly. These doubts, combined with his natural dread of speaking out, prevented Johnny, when he was admitted into the study, from saying what he had come to say. The tobacco-laden atmosphere, the dark unreadable books, the guillotine, were all too much for his courage and instead, in shame, he told Mr Victor that he thought Edwardes seemed happier now.

This was true. After his experience at the pool Edwardes seemed to have attained as much emotional and mental equilibrium as nature had destined for him. He had given up the practice of which Johnny had been a reluctant witness in the kitchen garden of praying for his enemies in the solitude of his dank niche. Although in his scruffiness and disorganisation he was the despair of matron and master alike and although he continued absurdly boastful about his family there was not that special quality to his behaviour that invites the malevolent attention of fellows. When the communal spirit now required a scapegoat it looked elsewhere than at Edwardes. The strange boy's resurrection was due not least to the fact that, as somebody had remarked and as Edwardes now proudly reflected, he was the only boy in the school who had been off the high diving board at the pool.

Johnny's pride in his own part in Edwardes' recovery nowhere near offset the shame at his own failure to act on his decision to tell Mr Victor about Marvell's allegation. And he had to live with it, to live not only with the failure but with the knowledge that he was letting Marvell down as well as failing as Head of School. It was a bitter time for him when it should have been a good one, not only because of the glow of his exhibition but because Mr Victor now announced the Mikado plan. The boys generally knew little about – if indeed they had ever even heard of – Gilbert and Sullivan, but it was clear from the portentousness of Mr Victor's announcement that this was a considerable enterprise and so *The Mikado* rapidly passed into general conversation as the great event of the future, its image of course enriched by its association with the most glorious phrase in school vocabulary: 'the end of term'.

Johnny did not relish his part as the wandering minstrel, required as he would be, he guessed, to wear tights and sing love songs. He envied those like Tom Bennett who were able to make a vital contribution without embarrassing self-exposure by helping on the technical side of production. Not that there was a great deal of work in that respect for the lights consisted of a length of boxed footlights, four one-hundred-watt bulbs reflecting off silver paper. Nor, the stage being small and curtained on three sides, was there space for scenery or set. A chair or two and perhaps a table was as much as the stage could hold if two or more characters were going to be able to move on it with any freedom

The Mikado, however – this bold new enterprise – demanded something more ambitious. On display to everyone's admiration were the sketches Mr Blackstone had done for the design of the set. There was to be at the back, instead of the plain black curtain screening the rear wall, what was now grandly called a 'cyclorama'. This was to consist of a number of superannuated bedding sheets tacked together and painted with an appropriate oriental scene. In fact Mr Blackstone had taken as his inspiration the famous willow pattern design commonly seen on crockery. But this was not all: there was talk of extending the stage forward beyond the line of the proscenium arch (another new term for the boys) formed by the two stage curtains in order to create an acting space large enough for two choruses – the male and the female – in addition to the main characters. But most thrilling of all was the intention actually to build – not merely to depict on the cyclorama – a wooden bridge that forms a central and focal part of the famous willow pattern scene. This would stand stage-centre diagonally and frequent, in Mr Victor's imagination, were to be the passings over it, the lingerings and leanings upon it, on the part of the cast. The task of building this bridge and the stage extension would fall upon the artisanship of Mr Denman who braced himself for it with some pride and an equal reluctance to embark upon it.

So much for stage and set: what about the theatre itself? The Dell did not, of course possess a theatre as such but it did have a room of sufficient space for the purpose. This – designated the New Hall by Mr Victor but the Hut by everyone else – was a wooden building separate from the main school. In Mr Victor's mind it constituted an important phase in the school's development, symbolizing the need both to expand and to extend the range of facilities. In addition to being theatre it was assembly hall and exam room, spare classroom and gym. Not that it was any more than perfunctorily, if at all, equipped for any of these functions, possessing only the base staging at one end for drama with an upright piano to one side of it for assemblies. There were no gymnastic features like wall bars or anything of that kind.

It would anyway have been rash to have boys scaling the walls for the Hut, though of quite sizeable dimensions, was not very robust. It had nothing approaching the grandeur or durability Mr Victor would have liked for his first adventure in development but it had been more or less donated to the school by a benevolent parent whose trade included prefabricated wooden buildings. This Mr Dawson combined unashamed vulgarity of background and accent with blatant generosity that had Mr Victor at a loss as to how to respond except by graciously consenting to receive this gift-horse and thereafter doing his best to forget the lowly Mr Dawson's part in it. But the Hut was essential to the school's functioning.

❋ CHAPTER IX ❋

The Hut's frailty had been dramatically demonstrated on one occasion by Mr Ezzard, the boxing master. Boxing at The Dell was a minor sport of major importance: minor in the sense that it was voluntary, perhaps in deference to a growing popular feeling that has since wiped it off the sporting programme of every school in the country; major in the sense that Mr Victor attached great importance to it and put pressure on boys to participate. To him, two boys attempting to hit each other in a manner concordant with the famous Queensberry rules, was the ultimate in training for fitness and bravery – or manliness as his father would have called it. Boxing was a year-round sport – every Friday evening, in fact – and it formed the acme of the various contests of Sports Day. Its prestige was further enhanced by the employment of a coach, this Mr Ezzard.

No other sport in the school was in any sense coached. Football, for example, was a game you played according to certain rules; there were practice games on weekdays and matches on Saturdays, with little difference between these two other than that when Mr Victor shouted at you in a match he did so less offensively than in a practice game. But boxing was a more specialist sport in Mr Victor's mind and required specialist training: hence Mr Ezzard.

Mr Ezzard had spent the war years improving the fitness of

the nation's airmen, presumably so that they might the more vigorously press the bomb-release button when flying over enemy territory or, if unlucky enough to be shot down while doing so, then to be captured and imprisoned, that they might the more convincingly leap over vaulting horses while others – equally fit – dug escape tunnels beneath. Mr Ezzard's most athletic days were now over but he remained a tough man in prime condition for his years and nothing was lost of the energetic combative spirit that must have seen to it that numbers of the nation's airmen went to their deaths at the peak of personal fitness.

He would breeze into the Hut at the appointed Friday evening hour – never was there a moment's lateness to give encouragement to the waiting boys' wild dream that he might not turn up at all – and swing his bag of boxing gloves like a sack of scalps atop the old piano. These gloves, darkly stained with old blood without and pungently redolent of old sweat within were, to the boys, the instruments of shame, donned with distaste and apprehension, doffed with distaste and relief. Mr Ezzard would then select an unlucky pair of combatants of similar size and urge each to inflict maximum injury upon the other. The reluctant pugilists, however, being more intent on their joint self-preservation than Mr Ezzard was on their mutual destruction, generally triumphed over him by dragging their feet, feinting and feigning, equally uninspired by their trainer's bellicose exhortations as unashamed by his scorn of their pusillanimity.

Occasionally Mr Ezzard would himself 'take on' one of the senior boys. This was dreaded for although Mr Ezzard would talk instructively throughout the bout as if merely engaged in a little practical demonstration he would at the same time be landing shrewd and frequent blows on his luckless sparring partner whom he would simultaneously urging to a pugnacious response. While that poor boy's swings and jabs lost their force in the air or on his opponent's iron rib-cage Mr Ezzard's blows were rendered all the more forceful by the fact that he wore not conventional boxing gloves but a pair of leather mittens only slightly padded.

The evening would be rounded off with a session of the medicine ball. This was a curious object, acquired by Mr Victor at the prep school sale where his bids had secured for The Dell its initial equipment such as desks and Latin grammars, about the size of a large beach ball. It was leather-covered and padded like boxing gloves but it had something solid at its centre for it was very heavy. The boxers would gather in a circle and the ball would be tossed from one to the next. Any person dropping the weighty object was 'out'. Why it was called a 'medicine ball' no one knew, but Mr Ezzard, concluding a satisfactory evening by knocking the last remaining boy off his feet with it, clearly set considerable store by its use.

But to return to the matter of the Hut's frailty: one boxing evening Mr Ezzard, breezy as ever in his habitual white polo-neck jumper, demonstrated the pull-up by lifting himself on one of the low beams with which the roof of the Hut was trussed. This strain the single beam was quite well able to bear but when he started swinging while suspended from that beam the entire building began not only to creak but perceptibly to sway. It was not as if anyone thought the building would actually fall down but its limitations were in future recognised for the boxing boys' gleeful account of this phenomenon – embellished with incidentals like the swinging of light bulb flexes and the ominous sound of splintering – reached the highest level of common knowledge.

These limitations were to no one more apparent than to anyone attempting to produce a play in it, more particularly to anyone attempting, as Mr Denman eventually began to do, to build a stage set. Having brought in the quantities of wood required for all his work – timber scavenged from various corners of the school – Mr Denman found nowhere to put it that was not in his own or someone else's way; nowhere to work that was light, safe and convenient; nowhere to store his tools when not in use that the boys could not borrow or break them; and only after the direst threats could the small boys be prevented from using the incomplete bridge (when inverted) as a see-saw. Considerable excitement attended these unusually early preparations, 'For', as Mr Victor explained to the assembled school in the Hut one morning, 'the play this year is not only of a new kind but will be presented in a new way: at the end of term as usual but also, along with the final of the house boxing competition, on Sports Day in a month or so' – not the whole production of course but a selection of songs from the operetta which by then Mr Blackstone's singers were to have mastered.

Now, Sports Day. For while rehearsals and set-building were under way so well in advance the next most important event of the term was looming more closely.

'I don't really like Sports Day,' confided Balmforth to Johnny one evening as the two most senior members of the school exercised their public spirit by cutting long grass in readiness for the great day. Johnny with the broken-, Balmforth with the short-handled hook they swiped with only modest effect at huge tussocks of cocksfoot that had been allowed to enjoy rampant growth since exactly a year previously.

'I certainly don't like long distance,' agreed Johnny, for it was in order to create the quarter mile track that they were now labouring. Their initial assault would be followed by Mr Denman with the rotary mower. In another corner of the field that same stalwart was shoving and yanking at that same mower with the irritable urgency of a man who knows that when he has finished this job he has a happy hour or two of set-building to follow. Around these three labourers carefree boys played ball, climbed trees and called to one another across a balmy evening.

Johnny had already spent a fair amount of time that day on the same job – during the Latin lesson, in fact, for now that he had won his award and his classmates were preparing doggedly for the C.E., Johnny could be readily dispensed with for the majority of the lessons and put to more useful work. He was glad enough to escape class but it was lonely labour in which he had plenty of mental leisure to feel generally depressed about most things, including his failure to do anything about Marvell – and the longer he did nothing the less likely he was to do anything; including his unwelcome part in *The Mikado*; including his latent antagonism with Haines which, with the coming of Sports Day, was to take on a new edge for the following reason.

The school was divided for competitive purposes into two 'tribes', the Zulus and the Apaches. This arbitrary division set friend against friend, form-mate against form-mate; it stirred up otherwise quiescent passions of pride, envy, contempt and hatred; prompted acts of violence, cowardice and reprisal, as the result of which victors crowed and boasted while the victims glowered and grumbled. This spirit of healthy competition was rapidly wakening to life in the school as the Sports approached.

'Do you think we'll win?' Balmforth now asked Johnny, for they were both members of the same tribe, the Zulus, of which Johnny was chief. Chief of the Apaches was the inevitable Haines.

'Don't know,' Johnny replied, not wishing to reflect on their chances. Certainly Balmforth was not going to contribute much to their success, being slow and podgy. Throwing the cricket ball was the only event in which he might be expected to score his tribe any points.

'I say – crumbs – look at that!' Balmforth now exclaimed. In the centre of the field where the shorter distances would be run Haines was giving instruction to a number of younger boys in getting off to a good start in a sprint. 'He's training them!'

'Good Lord!' Johnny stared, incredulous. Coaching, as has been observed, was unknown at The Dell and here was Haines giving his men instruction and practice in 'On your marks' etc. For most boys it was sufficient to stand at the start and when the master said 'Go' to run: that was all there was to it. But Haines was getting them down on one knee and all that sort of professional stuff. Several Apaches were gathered round in respectful attention.

'Gosh, do you think we should do some of that, Clarke?' asked Balmforth.

'Don't be wet,' snapped Johnny, 'it's a complete waste of time.' But his heart raged within him, confronted thus with his two enemies: Haines and his own timidity.

But they were not alone in responding unfavourably to this caddish exercise on the part of the Apaches for suddenly a posse of middle-ranking Zulus burst out of the woods with wild cries and tore into their enemies, each with his own favoured method of inspiring fear in the hearts of the foe, some as machine-gunning fighter pilots, diving, dodging and ack-acking, others yelling and flailing their arms in an attempt to curdle blood. In no time it was a battle on a large scale, every member of the school instantly called to the colours by the inspiriting sounds of warfare, pouring in from all quarters and engaging without fear, yells of rage and pain intermingling with invocations to 'Kill them, Apaches' and 'Zulu, Zulu!'

This informal bout of inter-tribal competition was only put a stop to by Mr Denman's even louder command to desist. The combatants were dispersed to lick their wounds, record their triumphs and swear future retribution.

'That was pretty cowardly and pathetic, Clarke,' sneered Haines when only the two of them and Balmforth remained in the field.

'We didn't start it,' replied Balmforth. But Johnny knew it meant trouble.

It certainly lent a nastier edge to the house boxing competition that preceded the Sports Day proper. That Haines and Clarke would emerge as the finalists was a foregone conclusion at the outset. Throughout their time in the school they had been the toughest and fairest match in their year, sparring together Friday after Friday, each with his successes and sufferings.

It was not in the Hut that this competition was held but, the weather being fine, on the lower lawn. There all gathered, the fortunate non-combatants in eager expectation of violence and injury, the team-members – there were to be six bouts – mixing apprehension and determination. Now it had been Johnny's task as chief to select the Zulu team and this consisted – for want of better – of some rather unlikely characters. Balmforth, for reasons of total unsuitability, was not included but Edwardes was. Johnny just had this feeling that he might somehow make a fighter, being deep down very proud; he was also quite sizeable and had that violent, raging quality that might, if he were lucky with his opponent, be successful.

Alas! he was not lucky with his opponent: he drew Haines. Edwardes had been very reluctant to take part in the first place but Johnny had flattered and cajoled him. Now, as he sat and dumbly permitted the dreadful gloves – warmly damp inside with the exertions of the previous boxer – to be tied on to him such courage as he possessed deserted him in the face of his ancient enemy. He glowered in his corner till the bell rang.

'Good luck,' Johnny urged with desperate encouragement. He now had little hope. There was not only Edwardes' temperament against him and his total demoralisation over the identity of his opponent but also the fact that he was not amongst Mr Ezzard's pupils and had learned nothing whatever of the noble art. The staff attending – including Major Oakes, the referee – seemed blithely unaware that they were about to witness slaughter, but the avid onlookers knew that at least high drama and at most violence and bloodshed were in prospect. Nor were they disappointed.

In the dumb, still moment of waiting for the bell Edwardes had clearly decided upon his tactics, and they were simple: no sooner had gloves been initially touched than he shut his eyes and, feet planted firmly, set his arms into a rapid windmill motion. This flailing he sustained amid cheers and boos, for the whole of the first round (of three), while Haines danced ineffectually at a safe distance. In the second round he went into identical motion which he looked to be able to sustain throughout it, hoping, it was now clear, to survive the contest unstruck – though not of course by this means to win it. But

Haines could not let this be. Though in the first round it was the human windmill that drew the laughter, in the second his opponent began to look ridiculous in his inability to engage in combat. So Haines stepped in, to the renewed pleasure of the crowd, though with some caution, for Edwardes was clearly dangerous. He had to press on, however, or lose face, but his first determined assault upon his opponent nearly cost him the fight. Edwardes' windmilling action was continuing without variation and Haines walked into it as into the arms of a propeller, as indeed he was bound to do if he was to close with his opponent and get inside his guard (if such it could be called). Edwardes' right arm came down hard on Haines' left arm and the next moment his left fist came down heavily on Haines' right ear and thumped him on the shoulder. Haines staggered back to the delighted cheers of at least half the audience and nursed his discomfiture for what remained of that round.

It was different, however, in the third and final round for not only was Edwardes too tired to sustain his hitherto successful rotary action but Haines was angry and determined. A break in the rhythm of Edwardes' windmilling coinciding with a weakening of its power gave Haines his opportunity: he pounced – a swift left jab to the chest brought a grunting gasp from his opponent who now, suddenly quite defeated in spirit, hardly troubled to sustain a defence at all and was duly pummelled, jabbed and thumped by his relentless opponent. The Zulu cheering was turned to booing, the Apache booing to cheering and, Major Oakes intervening to prevent undue suffering, the fight was over, Haines hard-faced and triumphant, Edwardes panting and weeping silently.

'You didn't have to murder him,' Johnny reproached his rival chief later.

'He asked for it,' was Haines' glowering reply.

❧ CHAPTER X ❧

The eve of Sports Day; a long light evening; Johnny at work in his garden.
Frantic – as always – had been the efforts to prepare for the great day. The long-jump pit, its sand weedy and sunk in the middle like an old mattress, had been restored to golden evenness. The high-jump posts had been discovered in the games shed – though where on earth was the bar? Late into the long evenings had the tireless Mr Denman mowed and even Major Oakes had set to with a scythe and cut down a patch of nettles where the spectating parents were to be seated. A large number of chairs for this purpose had been transported on the school trolley and stacked under the oak tree against the threat of rain. It generally did rain on Sports Day; or it had done so sufficiently the night before to render the grass track slippery; or it showed every sign of being about to do so; or it rained enough to make participation and spectation alike unpleasant but not enough for Mr Victor to announce the entire event abandoned.

For this Johnny longed, having no relish, gifted though he was athletically, for sporting contests. Why did people have to throw themselves at things and at one another, he mused now, regarding with the deepest satisfaction the tiny green heads of peas that had just begun to sprout through the good earth? In the woods about him the usual cries of playing could be heard, as could the distinctive clank of the white-lining machine with which Mr Victor without aid of string unerringly ruled the delineations of the hundred-yard track. He would probably be wanting Johnny's help but Johnny had had enough of all that and felt quite justified in awarding himself a little peace and solitude before the great day.

Increasingly he loved his garden and had developed a fantasy based on it. It was easy to imagine from the crumbling and rank evidence still about him what a glory this kitchen garden must once have been. In his imagination Johnny recreated that glory: the three gnarled and leggy gooseberry bushes became a double row of six, six red, six green, the fruits so thick you could take a dozen in a single hand as they hung from the branches. On the south-facing wall the nectarine and peach trees stretched out their branches in parallel, ripe fruits shining at every node. Blackcurrants hung as big as grapes while scarlet strawberries nestled on their beds of golden straw. Long rows of spring cabbages grew hard and large as rugby balls. The dark green fronds of carrot gave promise of the crisp orange root below. There was enough parsley to cover an entire pig in the butcher's window and cauliflowers gleamed white and pure and round. The low box hedges were dense enough to rest a trug on. The roofs of the greenhouses were sprayed with distemper against the sun. Inside a long, dark, earthy-smelling shed pots stood on each other's heads like hats; tools of varying size and purpose hung cleanly from nails in the wall.

Such were some of the images Johnny created as he worked, seeing himself as simply and wholly bound into this rich process of nursing nature to happy fruitfulness, free from care, free from the world. The glow of his vision was intensified by the knowledge that tomorrow would bring people and shouting and contests: for him the responsibility of urging his tribe to a victory he didn't value and – worst of all – of himself fighting Haines in the boxing final, the last and greatest event in the whole day. That he could defeat Haines Johnny was sure, but he was equally sure that he had no real wish to do so. He lacked what Mr Ezzard called the 'killer instinct'. He was angry at Haines for having humiliated Edwardes but he did not think that that anger would be sufficient to spur him to victory in the great contest. It simply didn't matter as much as the beauty of the little pea sprouts pushing their heads through his rich soil.

Even as he was thinking this and strolling about his domain, Johnny's privacy and peace were broken by an angry muttering. In his former space between crumbling shed and water-tank Edwardes had again set up his altar of stone surmounted by bamboo cross. Here he knelt, a Book of Common Prayer open in his hands. Johnny's heart sank.

'I thought you'd given that up, Edwardes,' he said with a sigh.

By way of reply Edwardes raised his voice slightly. He was reading from the Prayer Book and the word 'cursed' received special emphasis in his recitation.

'Who are you cursing, Edwardes?' enquired Johnny.

'Who do you think?' Edwardes replied vehemently, his back still to Johnny, still kneeling.

'Cursing's not very Christian,' said Johnny.

'Oh yes, it is,' replied Edwardes triumphantly and he handed Johnny his prayer book over his shoulder without looking.

Johnny took the book. *A Service of Commination*, he read. He had heard of Communion and Confirmation all right but not Commination. ' "Cursed is he that smiteth his neighbour secretly", ' he read aloud.

' "Amen," ' responded Edwardes, adding ' "Cursed is he that taketh reward to slay the innocent".'

Johnny returned the book. 'Come on, Edwardes, this isn't going to do any good, is it?'

Edwardes rose and turned his eyes upon Johnny. 'Fighting wasn't much good, was it?' he demanded.

'You did hit him,' said Johnny lamely.

'And he hit me and won the fight,' replied Edwardes unanswerably. The cut lip, now swollen, testified to his suffering at the hands of Haines. 'I shall curse him till the day I die,' he said, glowering.

To Johnny Edwardes was – as to Haines – just crazy. But Johnny's soul recognised the truth of Edwardes' hatred. He felt drawn towards it. Edwardes had something to tell him that was true, something he must hear not just because it was true but because it would make a massive difference to him. Johnny longed not to ask the question that he had to ask.

'Why do you hate him so much?'

'Because he doesn't care if he hurts people,' replied Edwardes. 'He doesn't care. He doesn't like people. That's why everyone's afraid of him.'

'Everyone?' queried Johnny.

'That's why everyone hates him – because they're afraid of him.'

It was in Johnny's mind to ask 'Do you think I'm afraid of him?' but there was no need for he knew the answer. 'Of course I'm afraid of him.' And there was a terrible shame and humiliation in admitting it to himself. The shame was in recognising his own fear and in seeing how he had tried to conceal that fear. But instantly with the shame and the humiliation came relief and a great lightness of spirit for though there stood Fear to appal him it no longer lurked menacingly at the edge of his mind to diminish and disparage him – it was out in the open, albeit stark and terrifying. He knew now he would have to turn and fight it but he knew too that just as fear came out into the open, somehow or other courage had welled up in his soul to meet it. There was the Fear but here was the Courage. It was going to be a fair fight and mere defeat was the worst that could come of it. What did fear matter if it cast out Fear?

It was better, Johnny realised, to look Fear in the face than to let it threaten unseen.

He turned back to his garden, the golden dream faded. Instead Johnny contemplated Sports Day, let his mind rest on the coming combat, the fight between himself and Haines. Perhaps he would win, perhaps he wouldn't. It didn't matter:

he would do his best. He hadn't the killer instinct like Haines but he hadn't the loser instinct like Edwardes either. He would fight as best he could and no one would think the worse of him if he lost – someone had to lose. So it appeared it was not just Haines he was afraid of: he was afraid of failing, of losing face. Well now what a relief it was to feel it didn't matter. Now he would go into Sports Day afraid of his opponent but not afraid of Fear.

But what about other things in his life? Why had he not done anything about poor Marvell? The boy had turned to him for help as someone he trusted, as Head of School who had power and responsibility for others. And what had he done? Nothing. He had shied away from it, going to Mr Victor with the intention of telling and then backing out at the last moment. What was he afraid of? He didn't know – it was all very puzzling, but after that curious encounter with Edwardes Johnny felt that he must do something. He would do something as soon as possible. Not immediately of course and come to think of it, not tomorrow, Sports Day. He would speak to Mr Victor the day after. He must just check with Maxwell first to make sure of his story, then he would see Mr Victor and tell him.

In the morning, however, Johnny had changed his mind. He *would* tell Mr Victor about Marvell and Mr Blackstone without any further delay. It was more important than Sports Day. Johnny had awoken to a pure bright morning with the clear conviction that he must leave it no longer. Somehow his success that day depended on doing justice to Marvell and braving it out with Mr Victor. Accordingly at breakfast Johnny sought private interview with his headmaster. For the second time he entered the study with the same intent: this time he would not back out. Everything, however, was against him – he couldn't have chosen a worse time. Mr Victor was already dressed for the day in much the same attire as that in which he had quite recently taken a ducking in the river. Though his yellowing and baggy flannels seemed the droopier, his once gorgeous blazer more frayed, he had the voice of a man in firm control. Booming his 'Come in!' to Johnny's tentative knock he puffed energetically at his pipe and moved about the room in anxious search.

'See if you can find the big tape-measure, Clarke – it's about here somewhere. By the way, Mr Denman will probably want you at the long-jump pit, just to keep an eye on things – when you're not running yourself, of course, that is.'

'Yes, sir. Sir, I – '

'Has your tribe set out the chairs yet?'

'Yes, sir, we did that before breakfast.'

'Good. That's another merit point to the Zulus. Now is there something on your mind?'

'Well, yes, sir. It's not actually about Sports Day, sir, it – '

'Oh, good heavens, Clarke, in that case can't it wait?'

'I'd like to tell you about something that's happened, sir.' Johnny had taken courage from Mr Victor's still busying himself about the room: how much easier it was to broach something with someone when you didn't have to look them in the eye. 'It's about Marvell, sir. Well, it's about Mr Blackstone, really, I suppose.' He paused. Mr Victor straightened up and faced him, taking the pipe from his mouth.

'Well, what about Marvell? What about Mr Blackstone?'

'I don't know what to make of it, sir. It's just that Marvell seemed quite upset about it and didn't know what to do so I thought I'd better tell you.'

'But you haven't told me anything yet, Clarke. You're being quite incomprehensible.'

'Yes, sir.' Even now, Johnny realised, it was not too late. Mr Victor was attending to him but had not yet caught on to the seriousness of Johnny's information. If Johnny had said 'Oh, it's nothing really, sir' Mr Victor would have let him go, his own curiosity hardly aroused and only too glad to get on with his final hectic preparations for the great day's events.

'Well, what Maxwell said, sir,' Johnny went on, 'was that Mr Blackstone had...' Here the schoolboy slang-word 'fiddled' just could not be articulated in the solemnity of Mr Victor's study – 'had interfered with him.'

' "Interfered with him"?' Mr Victor seemed more puzzled than appalled.

'Yes, sir – touched him… you know, sir.'

'Touched him,' repeated Mr Victor quietly, at last perhaps begining to understand.

'Yes, sir, touched him' – Johnny hit brilliantly on the adult word – 'privately.'

'I see,' said Mr Victor, nodding. He put down his pipe and turned to look out of the window.

Johnny almost felt like dancing: he had done it! He'd been immensely brave – he'd told Mr Victor, told him quite clearly (in the end) and now the terrible burden of responsibility had shifted from his shoulders to those of Mr Victor whose blank back seemed eloquent of the weight that now sat upon it. He was free! He would tear into those sports like a man possessed; he would galvanise his team; he would sing those soppy Wandering Minstrel songs with all his heart and he would pummel Haines like a dynamo. Nothing could stop him.

Mr Victor turned and faced Johnny. There seemed now a darkness on the slack-jowelled face, his summer outfit seemed yet more drab and old. The vitality of a man going into combat had faded from him.

'Are you saying,' he articulated slowly, 'that Mr Blackstone acted improperly towards Marvell?'

'Yes, sir.'

'That there has been something… something physical in the relationship?'

'I think so, sir. That's what Marvell seemed to be saying. Of course I'm only saying what Marvell said – I don't know myself, sir.'

'I see.' Mr Victor moved slowly back to his pipe on the desk and began to disembowel it with a small metal instrument designed for the purpose. 'What was the word Marvell himself used?' he went on. 'You said 'interfered with'. Was that

Marvell's phrase?'

'No, sir.'

'Then how did he express it?'

'He said 'fiddled', sir.'

Mr Victor sat at his desk, nodding slowly. 'You have not told anyone else of this, Clarke?' he enquired.

'No, sir.'

'Well, keep it to yourself. I shall probably have to ask you more about it later. You may go now.'

Johnny went, hardly able to restrain himself. His descent down the banisters was swift and sure. He felt like a winner.

❋ CHAPTER XI ❋

One of the features of Sports Day was bonnets. When selecting the school's uniform on its foundation Mr and Mrs Victor had been inspired to design an article of headgear other than the conventional school cap which was worn on Sundays and at away matches. This article was intended to combine utility with formality, providing not only that extra touch of class on Sports Day – which should impress parents – but also save their wearers from the heatstroke that they would otherwise certainly suffer on an English May afternoon.

The bonnets were made of grey felt with a gold satin ribbon round the crown. They were rounded on top with a floppy brim. Being thus constructed they did not, like caps, convert readily to missiles and they could be subjected to the greatest indignities and yet be restored to something like their intended shape. To the boys these girlish articles would have been objects of hatred had they not been objects of derision. They were worn solely on that day and therefore enjoyed each year a certain novelty.

Mrs Victor's Sports Day energies were directed largely to ensuring that these bonnets were properly used: not for storing sweets conserved previously by non-participants against the tedium of the day, nor for collecting daisies, catching butterflies or for sitting on. Boys complied cheerfully with Mrs Victor's orders but not for long: dogs don't like ribbons round their necks.

It was a mark of Johnny's distinction in rank that he was implicitly excused the wearing of a bonnet. The absence of this indignity gave him more confidence in leading and encouraging his tribe and in helping to manage the occasion. He also enjoyed the extraordinary privilege of free movement about the field, the common herd being penned behind ropes in a small enclosure where they did experimental things to their bonnets and one another, being released only when called upon to step out for their event by Major Oakes' megaphone. Most of the boys had been knocked out of the competition at an earlier stage and were condemned, bonneted and whites-wearing though they were, to an entire afternoon of non-participation until the final event – the Rush – a race in which any who had not so far performed might do so. This, preceded by the brothers and sisters race – itself a source of much hilarity and not a few tears – formed the culmination of the athletic events. With its characteristics of jostling, tripping, bumping, calling out of facetious encouragement etc. it constituted the least dignified but most enjoyed part of the day.

But the afternoon began with more serious events when earnest finalists for the under-11 220 yards race, say, competed for coveted tribe points. Partisan yelling from the enclosure was without confine as the contestants ran for the tape. Major Oakes was ceaselessly calling competitors for the next race and announcing results for the last. Balmforth, assisting Mrs Logsdon, was privileged to sit at a table beside a blackboard on which were recorded in chalk the rising tally of points achieved by the two tribes. Mr Blackstone officiated at the jumping events that seemed to drag on undramatically for ever while Mr Denman, with both whistle and stopwatch hanging round his neck, strode officiously about in charge of all.

Mysteriously to the boys the parents seemed less caught up in the intensity of the proceedings than they might have been. Many of the chairs so scrupulously and numerously laid out in the former nettle patch by the Zulus that morning were empty. Some parents talked to each other during the races and their cheering was pathetic, though occasionally a devoted father would step out with a camera, before being frowned back into place by Mr Denman. Johnny's parents usually appeared for the latter part of the afternoon and the speeches. Johnny's father had on one occasion actually been the guest of honour and made the speech, to Johnny's embarrassment.

Busy as he was with his own events and with urging on his tribe, Johnny nonetheless cast an occasional glance in the direction of Mr Blackstone and Mr Victor in case something had 'happened' there. Was Mr Victor eyeing Mr Blackstone quizzically? The latter was slumped in a director's chair – his own – in a panama hat beside the high jump, calling out names of hopefuls who one after another approached the bar with all the caution of those who know that the main object of their activity is not so much to jump high as to land not too uncomfortably on the other side, since nothing but the ground was provided to cushion the fall of the descending athlete. But Mr Blackstone looked the picture of composure. Mr Victor himself seemed to have regained some of his Sports Day bustle in chatting to parents and interfering in the organisation.

So the afternoon's events wore on to their conclusion and as they did so the excitement rose, for Fortune, favouring now one tribe, now the other, seemed to have come to rest in the middle. If Junior Apaches had won their 100 yards, the Junior Zulus had won throwing the cricket ball; equally, while the senior Zulus had triumphed in the quarter mile the Senior Apaches had come first in the long jump. An urgent recount was called for, Balmforth – as possibly biased – was stood down from the score table by Major Oakes who joined Mrs Logsdon to check the figures. The excitement of the Rush – the result of which did not contribute to the score – was quite lost in the excitement of the recount. At one point all the staff were gathered about the score table. Then, when the checking had been done with all the scrupulous thoroughness demanded by the weight of the matter, the staff moved away and it fell to Major Oakes to make his final announcement to the effect that the number of points on each side was indeed equal and that therefore the outcome of the entire Sports Day depended on the result of the final of the boxing competition which, as everyone knew, was between the chiefs of the two tribes and would take place, as usual, after the songs and the speeches.

But then how – a murmur quickly arose – could the guest of honour present the Sports Day cup if its winner were unknown? Mr Victor and Mr Denman went into earnest colloquy and the matter was settled thus: though reluctant to depart from tradition and to defer the all-important prize-giving it was nevertheless essential that the winning tribe should be determined before the climax of the afternoon. The order of events would thus be as follows: tea on the lawn, followed by songs from The Mikado, followed by the crucial boxing match, followed by speeches and prize-giving.

Johnny had succeeded through the afternoon in keeping the thought of the boxing match at the back of his mind, for although some of the courage engendered in him by Edwardes the evening before remained with him now he was not at all keen to conflict with Haines whose killer instinct would be at its most murderous pitch on account of the importance of the outcome of the contest. Nor was he keen to do so in front of large numbers of parents and screaming boys. Yet again, it seemed to Johnny, everything depended on him.

A certain dampening of spirits, however, was not confined to Johnny for the weather had changed. A bright May morning had clouded over to threaten rain. By the time the hungry hordes had devastated the tea provided on the lawn a convincing drizzle had set in so that Mr Victor and Mr Denman were again in serious conclave and a further announcement was made to the effect that the remaining events would take place in the New Hall. Although this seemed to several parents ample justification – swiftly exploited – for an early return home large numbers trooped undeterred and accompanied by smaller sons and daughters to the Hut which, with the entire school in addition, was full almost to bursting.

These hundred bodies were, however, soon disposed about the space available to hear the Mikado songs. The singers were set on the stage, the boys seated on the bare boards (only slightly cushioned by their bonnets now that these were no longer required to keep out the rain) and the parents seated on the chairs which had been hurriedly transported thither from the sports field.

Mr Victor introduced this novel element: 'As you know, our school year comes to its triumphant conclusion with The Play. The Play has been a feature of The Dell since its foundation but this year we intend to go one better, as you may already have heard, and do a musical show. It is to be Gilbert and Sullivan's *The Mikado*. I shall as usual be producing and for musical reasons have also decided to take the lead male part – we are a little short of baritones amongst the boys at present' (laughter) 'and Mr Blackstone will be responsible for the music. It is to hear some of that music that we are now seated expectantly. Mr Blackstone – whose standards as you know are of the highest – has asked me to say that while we will all do our best we are at an early stage of rehearsal and perfection of performance must not be looked for'. (sympathetic laughter).

Johnny knew that his own part was very far from perfection. He had had barely fifteen minutes with Mr Blackstone on the solo he would be singing; he didn't know the music and he didn't know the words. Nor did he much like the song. As Mr Victor spoke he felt sick with apprehension at the combined trials of singing and boxing. At least neither of his parents had appeared.

'Nor,' Mr Victor continued 'will our performers be in costume.' He pointed, amidst further laughter, to himself and the damp little troupe of singers on the stage, all of them still in their Sports Day dress of white singlet and shorts, all of them standing in attitudes as natural as possible on, behind, in front of and generally around Mr Denman's willow pattern bridge, an item of the set to which Mr Victor proudly drew attention.

The musical entertainment began with a shortened form of overture, Mr Blackstone thumping earnestly away at the piano. A suitable atmosphere of pleasurable expectancy having thus been established in the room, the songs began, Mr Blackstone with difficulty playing and at the same time communicating with his singers, whose confidence and timing needed all possible support and direction. Nor was the quality of sound improved by a deepening drumming of rain on the roof, one or two members of the audience glancing up as if expecting to see the source of the sound or uncertain as to the roof's ability to keep out the downpour.

Inexorably, the chorus having done one turn and Mr Victor one of his solos, Johnny's turn came. He stood alone, bare-kneed, clutching his sheet of music which seemed to be shaking. That he was a wandering minstrel he duly if not very powerfully asserted; he testified a little more strongly to the shreds and patches he was to be dressed in and was then just moving a little more confidently, having got into the swing of it, into telling of the ballad-songs and snatches in which he traded when something occurred to distract him. The door at the far end of the hall facing him opened and in came his father. This was disconcerting enough in itself but much more so was the fact that he was accompanied by two policemen.

Concentrating on his song as he was, Johnny had no mental leisure to ponder the possible significance of this entry. However, his song soon came to a welcome conclusion to warm applause and he was free to speculate. Had his father brought these policemen with him? If so, what on earth for? Had they brought him; if so, ditto? If they had come at the same time as his father coincidentally still there remained the question 'why?'. Johnny's father stayed at the back of the hall with the two officers who stood, largely unnoticed by the parents who were facing the opposite direction and invisible to the boys even if they turned round, like commissionaires at the door – and was looking with earnest intent, Johnny thought, at Mr Victor beside him on the stage. As the next item began Mr Victor stepped off the stage to make his way in as casual a manner as the crowding permitted to the back of the room, there to get into earnest conversation with the three recent entrants. Johnny knew that the police had a number of duties and that they could have come on the trivial errand of informing someone he had parked his car in a dangerous manner or the solemn one that a boy's father had been killed in a road accident. The conversation was short and all four left unobtrusively through the same door.

Surely, Johnny thought, Mr Victor could not already have reported Mr Blackstone's fiddling Marvell, with the police on the doorstep to arrest him. And yet in Johnny's mind the police were connected with the crime that he knew Mr Blackstone to have committed. Some confirmation of this connection was produced when, at the conclusion of the songs and in the general melee that followed, Mr Victor returned and, after a word with Mr Blackstone, accompanied him out, all this unremarked by the audience but keenly observed by Johnny.

Then a mighty blast on Mr Denman's whistle and the dread announcement 'Ladies and Gentlemen, Boys – the next event is the final of the tribe boxing competition. We will clear a space and...'

Johnny's stomach lurched: now he was for it.

✻ CHAPTER XII ✻

To accommodate the fighters the space formerly occupied by squatting boys was noisily cleared as they moved up on to the stage where they jostled for the best positions from which to watch the contest. The front edge of the stage formed one boundary of the ring, Mr Denman chalked off on the floor its opposite side, while the two side walls of the hut constituted third and fourth. A chair for each combatant was set at diagonally opposing corners; the gloves – sweaty and bloody – were fetched; Balmforth, Johnny's self-appointed second, had procured a bucket of water and face flannel, together with a towel: that would teach Haines for training people.

The atmosphere in the hut was thick – in two senses. First, the number of bodies in it naturally caused a rise in temperature which combined with the dampness of most people's clothing after the drizzle to create a sweat-inducing humidity. This was in no way reduced by the total absence of ventilation in the building other than that created by the occasional opening of the only door, for though the designer of this simple construction had not overlooked that necessity, he had made the windows capable of opening only as to their top quarters which were small and made to be held open by a standard device involving metal arms with holes regularly spaced in them through which a pin in the nether part of the window would be fitted in order to hold the outwardly opening part at the desired angle. This metal arm had, however, at an early stage of the Hut's use been discovered to be of some metal far from robust and had therefore been snapped off and carried away for other, improper purposes. Consequently the little windows, though they could be opened, could not be held open.

No less intense was the emotional atmosphere. For all but two members of the school the day's exertions were over and nothing remained but the pleasure of watching their leaders inflict suffering on one another. And of course the outcome of the contest decided the winner of the day's cup: it could therefore not be more crucial. There was already some preliminary cheering even as the combatants made ready, cheering reinforced by thundering of feet on boards and rhythmic cries of 'Zulu, Zulu', drawn out on its long repeated vowel, syncopated haphazardly with the shorter, sharper amphibrachic 'Apache, Apache!' Many parents still remained, partly magnetised by their sons' intense involvement, as well as the guest of honour with Mr Victor (recently returned) at his side.

Mr Victor, Johnny could observe, was not his usual commanding self. Though he was exchanging pleasantries with his guest he looked very ill-at-ease and the sweat visibly trickled down his face. Neither Mr Blackstone nor the policemen had returned. But for further speculation on that matter Johnny had no leisure as Mr Denman's bell rang and the first of five rounds began. Jumping to his feet with what he intended to look like confidence-inspiring eagerness, Johnny had the extraordinary sensation that he would fall over immediately and never rise again. But his legs upheld him and he circled cautiously his wily-looking foe. Haines peered over his bobbing gloves as over a mobile rampart, his skinny elbows ready to drop at an instant's notice to the defence of his ribcage, the fists themselves swaying slackly like cobras ready to strike. The first round was uneventful, each combatant slow to launch an offensive, anxiously weighing up the opposition. Of course the two had met before under Mr Ezzard's bloodthirsty tutelage and each was aware of the other's strengths and weaknesses: while Haines was fit and nimble, Johnny was weightier and struck a harder blow.

'Get into him, Clarke!' urged Balmforth as he fanned his champion at the end of round one. 'Give him what for!' Such amateur exhortation was of little value but Johnny did recognise that he must begin to use his weight soon before it became a burden to him and he slowed down, perhaps dropping his guard to Haines' deft jabs. At the very outset of round two Johnny began to crowd his opponent, his left thumping in even if it was only into those defending gloves, his right looking for an opening. Haines began to jab back and at last they were beginning to hit – their moves were quicker, the blows were landing and the boards squeaked under their dancing gym shoes. The cheers rose – to Johnny a senseless indistinguishable yelling that nonetheless kept him bobbing and striking, his opponent no longer a person but an abstraction, a job to be done.

With the third round the intensity increased – nearly half way through the fight and as yet no indication of the superior. Again Johnny weighed in, now a little more anxious to land those blows, a little less careful to keep his guard. Haines was looking flushed, a dark red patch on his neck; Johnny himself had sustained a painful blow direct on the nose. They fought on.

Round four was much as round three, each boxer the more anxious to make his impact but still, as the cheering intensified, there was no sense of the battle going one way or the other. The fifth and final round opened to a deafening cheer, the onlookers almost as red and sweaty as their champions, as the leader of the Zulus rose for the final assault upon the leader of the Apaches. But it was to no avail: each summoned up unknown reserves of energy and concentration to outwit and outstrike the foe; each defended as solidly as he attacked aggressively and though some blows were landed sufficient to give one tribe or the other cause for a new outburst of cheering there was no sense of one landing more, or more effectively than the other so that when Johnny, the last bell having sounded, slumped exhausted into his chair and submitted to Balmforth's ministrations of water and towel, he was convinced that he was neither a winner nor a loser. What would the judges make of it?

The judges – Mr Victor and Mr Denman – went into serious conclave. Silence had had to be called for so that they might hear each other – a silence that after the cheering fell, along with a drizzling patter on the roof, with an immediate intensification of the atmosphere, now, in both senses, unendurably thick. The unopened windows ran with condensation; boys, visibly steaming like cattle after rain, fanned themselves with their bonnets; formally dressed parents doffed outer garments, loosened ties and mopped brows with handkerchiefs. The judges' consultation continued; they compared notes, nodded, shook their heads; eventually they separated and Mr Denman, sounding his bell, stood apart to deliver judgment. Thus: 'The judges have decided,' he declaimed as portentously as the extraordinary occasion demanded, 'that in the absence of a knockout and with the battle honours so equally divided between them' – (cheers, booing, laughter and stamping) – 'it is impossible to declare either one of the contestants the winner.' (Clamour overwhelming) 'Both fought so well that it would be quite unjust to either if the laurels were awarded to one or the other just on the strength of it. Accordingly' – (pause for din to subside) – 'accordingly, to bring things to a conclusion the matter will be decided as follows: the leaders of the two tribes' – (deafening partisan applause) – 'will, having battled it out indecisively with the gloves, now battle it out decisively with the medicine ball' (loud cheers). Then, holding that curious leather pumpkin aloft with his one hand – most boys could barely sustain it in two – Mr Denman explained how. 'Standing behind this line,' here he chalked one in the former boxing ring, 'the chief of the Apaches will throw the ball to the chief of the Zulus standing behind this line' – here he chalked another. 'The ball must be thrown so that it can be caught. A mis-throw will cost the thrower the competition and therefore the Sports Day cup. Equally, to drop a catch is to lose. The chalk line must not be crossed. May the best thrower win!'

This sudden-death competition put the boys into a state of nearly uncontainable hysterics – for this whole vital issue could be decided by a single throw – as their leaders grimly took up their stances behind their lines. A coin was tossed for the starting advantage and Johnny was the first to feel that terrible weight thumping into his chest and to enclose it in his arms. In return he got his hands beneath it and shoved up and away at his opponent.

With each discharge a mighty roar arose. All now – parents included – were on their feet, thronging closer to the scene of the action. Then, somehow spontaneously, the bodies of the crowd began to sway from side to side in unison with the great leather ball. First this way, with a crescendoing cheer, then back with another, swayed the bodies, those standing by the walls crushed against them, to be released as the ball returned. Unnoticed in the excitement, the light bulbs too swung on their flexes; unheard, the walls, mere timber and hardboard, creaked and groaned. With each throw the swaying grew greater as the tension increased – how long could the two boys go on? – and the spectators at last found a way of sharing in this crucial action, of adding their bodies to their voices.

But as the power and the passion of the crowd intensified so Johnny felt his own diminish. How many more times could he embrace this thumping weight that crashed into his chest with breathtaking force? It was now almost all he could do to get his hands under it and heave it the necessary ten feet at his opponent. The sweat was running into his eyes, he could barely breathe, his arms were turning to sand. As he should have done in the boxing match he must now, he realised, go all out for victory. And with that decision came a sudden inspiration. The next time, as the great object crashed into him, he summoned up all his remaining strength and instead of preparing to push it back away from his chest he went up on tip-toe, thrust it up past his face and above his head, balancing it there for a moment – for he had no grip at that angle – and then, letting it begin to fall forward, got his hands behind it and brought it down upon his opponent with every ounce of power left in his mind and body. Carried forward with the effort, all the bodies in the room swaying in sympathy with him, he crashed prostrate upon the boards just short of the crucial line. That was it – make or break – for he knew he would be unable to get back up in time to collect Haines' return. But while that throw had been his last effort so it proved to be the last blow for Haines. Bracing himself for this newly angled and descending weight Haines staggered on its impact and stepping back rapidly to regain his balance was committed to a little totter backwards, the issue uncertain with every step as to whether he would gain equilibrium and stand firm, the ball safely in his arms, or whether he would be overwhelmed and fall over on his back. As he reached the wall behind him, still propelled helplessly by the impetus of Johnny's mighty throw, that issue remained undecided and he crashed against the hardboard with combined weight of body and ball. At the same time all the sympathetically swaying bodies of the spectators hit that limit too and there was a loud crunch that betokened more than a simple impact. Suddenly aware of the Hut's structural frailty the crowd went still, the light bulbs alone swaying. A terrible hush of suppressed panic electrified all in the building. Then after that first alarming crunch a further creaking was heard and to the astonishment of boy and parent alike the whole building began to keel, walls and the roof with them tipping gently over to crush them all. If stillness could have saved them it must have done so: they held their breath. It was as if the Hut were a boat that just another inch of incline will send plunging to a fatal capsize and sinking, or a vehicle that has come to rest on a cliff's edge, swaying there, infinitesimally balanced between stability and disaster: a feather could tilt the scale.

Every crisis brings forth its hero – sometimes an unexpected one. Mr Denman took command. 'Sit down carefully, everybody, slowly and cover your heads with your arms. Then keep still.' All, without murmur, obeyed. Mr Denman alone remained standing, even Mr Victor and the guest of honour having instinctively obeyed this voice of authority. Only Mr Denman could see that even if the building collapsed no further they were not yet saved, for the Hut in its five-to-ten degree lurch had jammed the door shut. How, therefore, could they get out? Fortunately at the stage end the inwardly-inclining wall was held to some extent by the (now not quite) upright piano on which Mr Blackstone had so recently been playing. That might be sufficient to prevent further collapse there but could it arrest the entire wall? And what about the other end? Mr Denman saw the answer. Stepping cautiously between crouching bodies he made his way to the stage and the willow pattern bridge that was to form the centre-piece of *The Mikado*. Hefting it solely with his one mighty arm he transported it the length of the Hut to the inwardly-inclining wall at the door end and leant it up against it like a buttress. Then, cautiously, he went to the door, turned the handle and pushed. Nothing. He pondered a moment, stepped back, clearing a little space for himself amongst the trembling bodies, and then, bowing his head as if in respectful obeisance, he charged the door like a bull, smacking it full-on with his forehead – the door swung open with a screech, there was a renewed crunch and crack as nails tore at their fixings, the building dropped a few more degrees then crashed to a stop, upheld by piano and willow-pattern bridge.

Mr Denman turned. 'Will everybody now leave the Hall please, one at a time, visitors first. No hurrying. Boys, stay where you are until the visitors have left.' Then he stepped outside the building to make way for escapers. The first one coming out to safety, Mr Denman swayed and – as the Hut most probably would have done but for his presence of mind, courage and resourcefulness – collapsed on to the wet grass.

PART TWO

CHAPTER XIII

'Bags I be Rat.'

'You look like one anyway.'

'Ha, ha, Morrison. You be the Mole – he's such a drip, Mole.'

'I want to be the Chief Weasel.'

'So do I!'

'Who wants to be Marigold? Who wants to be the *girl?*'

'Marvell can be the girl – he looks like a girl.'

'Bags I be Rat!'

'Bags I be Toad!'

'Fains I be the Washerwoman!'

'All right,' said Johnny loudly and authoritatively above the uproar. 'All right. Now listen. I'll decide who's going to be who.'

'Please, Clarke, can I be Rat?'

'All right, Davies. And Morrison, you're the Mole.'

'Yah-ya,' jeered Davies, 'told you so, Moly Morrison – what a wet!'

'Shut up, Davies,' warned Johnny, 'or I'll make you the barge-woman.'

'Cor! No fear! Rat has pistols and cudgels and everything,'

'Steady on, Davies,' said Johnny, 'we're only reading the play, you know – not acting it.'

Johnny began to regret his play-reading idea. He had thought as he came across the tattered and coverless copies of *Toad of Toad Hall* in Mr Blackstone's classroom cupboard that a bit of play-reading might keep this young form quiet or at any rate more amused than anything else he could think of. It was, apart from any other consideration, the only book of which Mr Blackstone's cupboard held more than five copies, with the exception of *Oliver Twist* of which there were fully thirty, of great antiquity and in spectacularly small print.

Of 4B Johnny had become, on the departure of Mr Blackstone, virtually form master. Having before half-term taken on a little pedagogy in recognition of his Worthington award, he was now more teacher than taught – in fact a week into the second half of term he had not received a single lesson, Mr Victor having abandoned even the occasional Greek session in order to bring up to scratch in Latin the row of duffers shortly to take C.E. How he was to improve his lamentable Maths in order to satisfy the headmaster of Worthington Johnny did not know; perhaps that was to be dealt with in September. Nor was it an issue Mr Victor had at the forefront of his mind, that position being fully occupied by deeper and more pressing concerns.

Not least of these was, of course, the sudden whisking away of Mr Blackstone by the police. In the ten days since that disastrous Sports Day Mr Victor had been informed that Mr Blackstone was being questioned with regard to an incident in the town's public lavatory and that charges might be preferred; that therefore his return to The Dell was unlikely. For all Mr Victor knew from then on Mr Blackstone might already be in jail or fined or let go with a caution – that did not concern him. What did concern him was the fear that the police might extend their investigations to The Dell, in which case the little red-haired angel, Marvell, could be relied upon in his innocence to sing like a canary – and if he, perhaps others, with possibly disastrous consequences for the reputation of his school. In addition to which he was now without a French and English and music master at a stage in the term when the chances of finding a replacement were minimal.

Talking of replacements, there was Matron too, for Matron's aunt, a dear old lady who had looked after her as a child and whose flagging health was a constant topic of conversation with her, had taken a severe turn for the worse and must be attended to. Mr Victor could not even attempt to resist her departure, Matron having stayed on from the previous term only on the understanding that such a call as this might come and must be met. She was so good a matron – motherly and efficient – that Mrs Victor had kept her on, hoping that the failing aunt would considerately delay her terminal decline until the summer holidays. The alternative, after all, was an impossibly increased burden for herself or the appointment of some feckless chit who didn't know a verucca from a chilblain and was not to be trusted with staff or boys.

Nor was there the slightest hope of ending the term with the dramatic flourish of *The Mikado*, for the double reason that he had lost in Mr Blackstone his co-producer and singing director, and, in the collapse of the Hut, both his theatre and the willow pattern bridge, presumed distorted beyond repair in its noble and life-saving role of Hut supporter in the moment of its otherwise certain and possibly fatal collapse. This disastrous event had of course been chronicled in the local newspaper which had sent a young reporter to record it. Such were the limitations of this photographer and his equipment, however, that any building he photographed looked as if it were leaning; hence his photograph of the inclining hut actually represented it as perfectly upright and it appeared in the newspaper to be quite a substantial building as well. It therefore put The Dell in not such a bad light as Mr Victor feared and it seemed a shame that it had to go. Mr Dawson, the parent in the trade who had made much of his original supply of it, was now less in evidence to give advice on its reparability or removal, so there, for the present, it leaned, strictly out-of-bounds and posing the problem not only of its replacement but also of its dismantling and the extraction of the piano plus numerous chairs, the latter much missed in the day-to-day running of the school, with boys sitting on classroom floors and window-sills until Mr Victor could think of a way of extricating them without expense, further damage or injury.

To the solving of this problem Major Oakes' mind was committed – surprisingly perhaps in view of Mr Denman's heroic action in ensuring the safe escape of parents and boys from the teetering structure. The truth was that since that significant episode and perhaps as a result of the extraordinary butting out of the door Mr Denman had been in a slightly bemused state and unable, it appeared, to engage mentally with the problem of what to do next. Perhaps inspired by Mr Denman's example Major Oakes now appeared ready to make his contribution to the affairs of The Dell.

'I suppose we could all kind of push it back up again, sir – I mean if we all pushed.'

This, the suggestion of one bright member of a small group (including Johnny) gathered, as there always was a small group gathered when free time permitted, simply to look at the ruin, to share reminiscences of the event leading up to it and to speculate on the building's future – this suggestion met with little favour.

'And stand there holding it up, I suppose,' responded Major Oakes tartly.

'Just an idea, sir.'

'Bloody silly one, Bancroft.'

'Yes, sir. Sorry, sir.'

The occasional swear-word that garnished Major Oakes' rather spare repartee gave the boys great pleasure, including them as it seemed to do in a manly world for which they were as yet unqualified and indicating the existence of moral standards – or immoral standards – far removed from those so piously advertised by their headmaster. Not that the boys themselves would have thought of uttering a swear-word for fear of the consequences, except in the dark privacy of a whispered late-night conversation in the dormitory. All the more did they warm their hands at the glow of Major Oakes' occasional verbal indiscretion.

'I've got an idea, sir,' piped another hopeful. No answer from Major Oakes. 'We could kind of pull it up with ropes from the other side…and then tie the ropes round those trees and then we wouldn't have to stand there holding on like in Bancroft's daft idea…and then we could get the chairs out and everything. Sir. Do you see what I mean?'

'How much rope do you think would be required, Coombes?' asked Major Oakes witheringly.

'Oh gosh, I don't exactly know, sir. I hadn't thought of that. I suppose – gosh, well – a couple of jolly long pieces, I suppose.'

'*Jolly* long pieces,' affirmed Major Oakes heavily, staring morosely at the Hut.

'Maybe Mr Bolton's got some rope, sir. Shall we ask him – see what he's got in his shed?'

This was something of a tease since, as the young speaker knew well, Mr Bolton was not one to be approached lightly even by a member of staff and certainly not with a request. Even Mr Victor, seemingly lord of all he surveyed, had long since learned that to get the best out of Mr Bolton – or rather to get anything at all out of Mr Bolton – one had to let him get on with it, 'it' being whatever (if anything) Mr Bolton felt like doing as and when he felt like doing it. This was not much, not often and not very well. There was the sweeping of the terrace, for example, which Mr Bolton did every Saturday morning with his home-made besom. That the terrace did not, even in autumn, require such regular sweeping; that the weeds in the flowerbeds alongside the terrace would be crying out for deracination; that Mr Victor would glower at him through the dining room window as he swept – such factors had not the smallest impact on Mr Bolton's routine. 'Well at least,' reflected Mr Victor – and the least was clearly what he was going to have to settle for – 'at least the terrace is always more or less tidy.'

'Clarke, you know about gardening and things,' Major

Oakes said, having obviously accorded this unsolicited suggestion the status of one at least worth demolishing in a practical way. 'Take me to Mr Bolton's shed.'

Major Oakes had spoken and suddenly excited by the possibility of action the group of idle onlookers became an animated retinue as Johnny led Major Oakes towards the kitchen garden, entry to which, it will be remembered, was permitted only to Johnny and in one corner of which was situated Mr Bolton's shed. The retinue, now increased in numbers as mysteriously as a rural crowd in the orient, was left reluctantly milling at the doorway into the sacred precincts, speculating on the chances of success of the search party while Johnny and Major Oakes marched in. It was well past the (very early) hour that Mr Bolton would be seen wheeling his ancient bicycle slowly out of the school grounds at the end of his day's labour, so there was no fear of encountering him or his obstructionism.

This was actually quite exciting for Johnny since, though this famous shed was never locked, he had never entered it, the few tools he used for his own gardening being broken and rusty implements that were simply leant against the wall when not in use. Mr Bolton's shed proved to have no more in it than the predictable tools of his trade stacked loosely against the wall or hung on nails and a potting shelf where a few pots lay amongst a small mound of earth. A glance showed that here was nothing of the kind required for their operation. But 'What's through there?' enquired Major Oakes, indicating a door at the end of the shed. Of course Johnny had no idea so they went over and Major Oakes pushed it open.

Even in the modern age of the DIY superstore there persists still the occasional little side-street hardware shop whose walls and ceiling are festooned with every imaginable device, receptacle, tool, part or fitment that the householder and handyman could require. What now met the astonished eyes of the two interlopers was just such an Aladdin's cave of artisan's equipment, though of course in its used rather than its new state. In contrast with the half-empty and tumbled look of the outer shed here, in a space much larger but one of which Johnny had been completely unaware, was fulness and tidiness, order and plenty. Here were long reels of wire of different thicknesses, here a garland of bath plugs; here boxes of nails and screws, neatly arranged along a work-bench above which hung a range of carpenter's tools all wearing a look of recent use; here were neat piles of wood for working, here bundles of coppiced hazel, tall and straight, bamboo of differing length and thickness; pots of paint, bottles of various liquids ranged on the shelves; sacks, bins, trugs and baskets; an axe and chopper hung together on the wall alongside a range of saws and a netful of wedges for splitting logs; paintbrushes large to small hung on hooks by holes in their handles. In one corner an old but commodious and fairly clean armchair afforded the proprietor a comfortable place beside a little enclosed coal stove whose tubular metal chimney made its way up into the roof, in the timbers of which large items such as a double-handled saw, ladders and a pair of wrought-iron gates were stored.

'Good God! So this is how the old bugger spends his day,' exclaimed the Major. The joy of the unfamiliar obscenity was lost on the equally astonished Johnny, at that moment distracted as he suddenly was by something particular he saw hanging on the wall: the most enormous coil of very thick rope.

❋ CHAPTER XIV ❋

Mr Victor's contribution to the progress of civilisation was to retard it as far as lay in his power. And of course within the school it lay entirely within his power since school was – to the boys at any rate – a sealed system: they did not go out except to church and to other prep schools and nothing came in – newspapers being seen by the staff only and the wireless unheard. Anything and everything of recent invention – be it idea or art form or technological development – was despised and ridiculed. In the pictorial arts, for example, while the Impressionists (initially derided by the establishment of their day, of course) were aesthetically acceptable after fifty years or so of familiarity, anything by Picasso was condemned as pretentious rubbish. Being himself of an entirely uncreative mind Mr Victor did not acknowledge creativity in others, poured scorn on enthusiasm and depreciated inventiveness. God's law and nature's law – and of course, society's law, which derived from them as laid down by an English historical process based on constitutional monarchy, parliamentary democracy, legal precedent and the Church of England – these ultimate laws had been firmly established ab initio and merely required dogmatic enforcement without the liberal fudge of interpretation, let alone modification.

Thus all that was done at The Dell was as it had always been done: times and seasons had their rituals, every observation of which entrenched and enriched their value. And the rapidly growing hearts and minds of his charges, swaying uncertainly in their ebullient growth, naturally twined themselves round these unchanging pillars.

The effect on his community of these ideals and standards was, however, not always of the kind hoped for. Thus, for example, since pederasty was quite unthinkable its reality in the person of Mr Blackstone went undetected by Mr Victor himself, blinded as he was by the brilliant purity of his vision, so that what was abhorrent to him flourished under his nose because of his own perverse innocence. In the same way he allowed boys (as has been told) two to a bed for his uplifting dormitory reading sessions, little conscious that the sub-text, as it were, of these sessions was in conflict with the overt narrative.

But on a less dramatic level the effect of his – as he saw it – courageous stance in the face of 'progress' (and no word carried on his tongue a more sneering intonation) was, on his staff, simply depressing. The potentially inspired passions of Mr Denman – witnessed in such momentary brilliance in his heroic action in the Hut – were stifled by the drudgery and repetitiveness of the prep school master's life. Witness also Major Oakes whose war-time MC, never publicly accounted for by him, was in unexplained contrast with his habitual moroseness and sarcasm: he must once have done something very brave but who would have thought it now? The staff were thus condemned to meeting the vitality of youth with the dying dogmas of middle age in an atmosphere of penny-pinching puritanism. Only for Mr Victor, as he re-bound for the third time an ancient set of Algebra textbooks rather than replace them, and for Mrs Victor, as she held back two eggs from the toad-in-the-hole batter-mix, did the whole regimen of restraint, correction, 'making do' and eking out carry any spiritual satisfaction. It was, after all, their business. And their intended route to business success was by means of minimal investment. Alas, this did not seem to be working, for business was not good; and where business was not good hatches must be battened down and belts tightened. To batten down and tighten the hatches and belts respectively of other people in one's own interests is not unsatisfying: involuntarily to have one's belts and hatches tightened and battened down is not.

'Let's take it,' therefore, was Major Oakes' decisive injunction born of natural rebellion as he too saw the luxuriantly plentiful supply of stout rope that was only one of the hoarded treasures of Mr Bolton's cave. Each with a coil over one shoulder Major Oakes and Johnny were accorded a warm reception by the patient retinue still hopefully loitering at the doorway to the kitchen garden. And the party was further augmented by the time it reached the Hut, a buzz of expectation at unusual goings-on having communicated itself around the grounds: the Hut drama, it seemed, was moving into another act, seats for which would be highly desirable.

Arrived at the Hut, however, Coombes' idea of re-erecting it by means of ropes was found to be somewhat lacking in detailed planning. To what exactly should the ropes be attached? And from where should they be pulled? – for the Hut was located at the perimeter of the grounds alongside a hedge away from which it was leaning. Those standing in school grounds were therefore in no position to pull.

However, Major Oakes' mind, normally quiescent, had by now been stirred by the unlawful appropriation of the rope and was quite capable of meeting the problem.

'Tie a rope round the window stanchion – the windows at either end,' he commanded. An explanation of the word 'stanchion' having been given and the job actually done by Major Oakes it was next necessary to 'Throw the whole rope over the roof.'

'What – to land in the hedge, sir?'

'That's right.'

'Supposing it overshoots and goes into the kennels, sir?'

For the school's neighbour on the other side of the hedge was a boarding kennels, the howling and yapping of whose inmates formed a constant auditory background to life at The

Dell. Although this hedge was thick – albeit reinforced by chicken wire – and the dogs generally unseen there were one or two places where thinner growth permitted communication between boy and dog. Boy had been known to exploit this opportunity out of boredom and to post through the wire some small edible offering. Since, however, living conditions at the kennels, including diet, were superior to those at The Dell this traffic was light and boy would more often resort to taunting for the pleasure of a loud barking reaction. This reaction would in turn bring the mistress of the kennels upon the scene in equally loud outcry followed by subsequent complaint to Mr Victor. On the whole, therefore, boys and dogs respected their barrier.

'Never mind that,' said Major Oakes, 'just bung it over, will you, Haines?'

The rope attached to the window at the right-hand end of the Hut was duly bunged. So vigorous had been the bunging, however, that its end did indeed overshoot and land in the kennel compound, provoking clamour from the inmates. The rope now lay across the roof of the Hut, straddled the gap between Hut and hedge and hung over its further side. A nimble boy clambering in the hedge was able to reach up and draw down the rope, thereby bringing it safely in from the neighbouring territory before the alarm was truly raised.

'Good show – now for the other one.'

But with number two – Johnny was in charge of the left hand end of it – the opposing eventuality was not envisaged: that the rope's end, instead of overshooting, should fall short. This, however, is what – alas – happened, for Johnny's rope was not only thicker but longer and therefore a good deal heavier and although he bunged it with all his might it travelled with inadequate force so that, far from hurtling over the hedge into the kennels, it plopped loosely and quite out of reach on the further side of the Hut roof.

'Weedy throw, Clarke!'

'You try.'

'Now what do we do, sir?'

The situation was, however, easily retrieved by pulling the rope back and re-coiling it for another throw. This Major Oakes undertook but with a similar result since he had no more strength than Johnny. The third throw achieving no better result, it was decided that someone would have to go up on to the roof of the Hut and drop the end down on to the far side.

Who more appropriately than the smallest boy in the school, Marvell? A ladder having been fetched from Mr Bolton's store Marvell ascended without hesitation, it being a paradox of his character that, though minute and tender, he was quite without fear as if no force, human or otherwise, would think of inflicting injury on one so flagrantly vulnerable and innocent as himself. Once aloft he looked about him with simple wonder.

'Cor! Things look all different from up here. I can see Mrs Bolton at the kitchen sink. I can see all the dogs.'

'Yes, yes,' said Major Oakes, 'now get on with it, Marvell.'

'Gosh, it feels quite wobbly up here, sir.'

'Then stop dithering about and chuck the rope end down on the other side. You there, Clarke?'

It was in truth an anxious phase of the operation for Major Oakes, the commanding officer. Sending a boy up on to the roof was risky in itself, though he had reasoned that in the event of the Hut's collapsing further Marvell would merely take a bit of a tumble rather than be crushed. Still it would be better to get that part of the operation done. And done it soon was, Marvell dropping the end of the rope down with solemn care before mincing delicately down the purloined ladder.

It was easy then to tie the two ropes round the trunks of stout saplings in the hedge and return these in the direction from which they were originally thrown so that they might be pulled on by willing hands, thereby re-erecting the Hut and effecting the rescue of piano and chairs. But of course pulling the Hut upright was one thing – holding it upright was another. Recourse was therefore again had to the now shamelessly pillaged Bolton store and a sledgehammer and iron posts brought forth in order to create a fixing point for the rope-ends. Iron bars sledge-hammered in, heaving on the rope was then the order of the day. Well in training in this activity following the Sports Day tug-of-war many hands gripped and feet braced themselves. Upright slowly inched the Hut amidst a low protestation of nails and timber.

'Hold her there – hold her steady,' commanded Major Oakes, resorting suddenly to jargon more naval than military, from his central position between the two gasping gangs of tuggers. 'Now lash her on, lash her on!' And the two ropes were frantically whipped around the posts angled into the ground like tent pegs and knotted safe.

'Whew!' They all stood back, panting, proud. There stood the Hut, as erect (nearly) as on its first day, the clever ropes arching over the roof from their window fixings and passing through the hedge to come back to their anchorage wide of the Hut's ends. There was little leisure, however, for complacent contemplation of this achievement. No sooner was Major Oakes' mind beginning to plan the safe extraction of the piano as the first priority – the school trolley having been brought for the purpose – than the ominous rending of wood was heard. At the right-hand end of the Hut the rope, when it had been returned from the direction of the kennels, had become somehow not fully extricated from the hedge and the chicken-wire reinforcement so that now under the immense tension of the Hut's weight and the iron-post anchorage a certain amount of relative slack was taken in and the Hut at that end gave a lurch back towards its former angle – to its former angle and indeed beyond, to the point where total collapse seemed imminent. But the left-hand end held. The Hut, however, as if determined in its own mind on self-destruction and baulked of a lateral decline, shifted inexorably from its skew-whiff stance into an endways tilt, and whereas its internal structure had helped prevent its fall in that direction no such strengthening existed to prevent its fall longitudinally. The left-hand end securely braced, the right-hand end slewed and bowed towards it, the whole structure suddenly screeching and scrunching to a collapse beyond the most optimistic hope of re-erection.

Fleeing to a safer distance, the heroes of this operation, now suddenly reduced to helpless spectators of a self-created disaster, could but stand and watch as the Hut settled on to the ground, almost with a gratified sigh as if achieving a position of comfort at last. The final note hanging on the otherwise silent summer evening was a gentle and not inharmonious twang from the now entirely shattered piano.

✳ CHAPTER XV ✳

The hell that there was to pay on account of this was duly paid by Major Oakes, not only to Mr Victor for the destruction of the piano and most of the chairs – though many had been rescued quite intact, others reparable, from the flattened ruin; but also to Mr Bolton whose indignation at the intrusion into his sacred shed and the unauthorised removal therefrom of certain items was muted by his own apprehension lest searching enquiry be made into the justification for his secret treasure-house.

Nor was that all. The betraying rope, coming loose somewhere in the hedge, had, unnoticed at the time, torn up the chicken wire that – rather than the hedge – actually restrained the neighbouring dogs. These, not slow to discover this fortuitous exit, made prompt use of it in considerable numbers as darkness fell, and long was the searching, loud the calling and endless the flashing of torches before every inmate could be recalled. So the mistress of the kennels extracted her due share of hell also and Major Oakes – his one foray into creative adventure having flopped dramatically – relapsed into his habitual inwardness: no MC this time.

Rock bottom in the fortunes of The Dell and of its ever-hopeful proprietor. But rocky though the bottom may be it is at least the bottom: one can go no lower, though this did not perhaps seem so to Mr Victor as he opened his local paper the following week to see a report – mercifully brief, accompanied by no photograph and with no mention of the subject's place of employment – that a Mr Blackstone of the town, a teacher, had been fined a certain sum for indecent exposure in the public lavatories. Emboldened by this, Mr Victor wrote to Mr Blackstone informing him that in the circumstances his services would no longer be required at The Dell. He paid his salary to the end of the month and sat back with something like a sigh of relief – albeit he was still short a French and English master.

It was not cheering, however, that a couple of days after the newspaper article appeared a certain parent – a butcher and local worthy with his ear to the ground – announced his intention to remove his eleven-year-old son at the end of term. He did not specify why but Mr Victor had his fears, not least that this tradesman might poison The Dell's name and perhaps contribute to its further decline in patronage by parents in Rotarian circles. Certainly this was not the social level from which Mr Victor aimed to draw his clientele but as things presently stood any clientele was better than none.

Nor, in spite of the way in which the Blackstone affair appeared to have settled, did Mr Victor feel at all easy at the prospect of an interview with Mrs Marvell. Mrs Marvell was not the sort to write and request a meeting at Mr Victor's convenience: she telephoned to say she was coming down the next day. This at least gave Mr Victor little time for indulging his apprehensions lest young Marvell had during the half-term weekend spilled the beans about Mr Blackstone's interference with his person.

She came in the Daimler and instantly put Mr Victor's palpitating heart at rest by bouncing in through the front door and embracing at random any child who came within her range including her own son whom she resembled in being diminutive and a redhead. In an age of austerity Mrs Marvell was a personification of affluence, her gorgeous self in all the greater contrast with the plainness of The Dell. She looked as if she had walked out of a fashion store – even her face looked as if it had been bought – and a powerful aura of scent wafted about her, lingering in whatever space she vacated in her rapid progress, for she was never still and never silent, her cheery monologue absorbing without hesitation anyone else's conversational contribution as it plunged on.

The drabness of the school impinged on her not at all as if the roseate glow in which she permanently lived suffused her surroundings also. Her pleasure in being herself extended to pleasure in whatever place she found herself – she'd have hooted and frolicked in a prison camp.

'Dear Mr Victor, how well you're looking – and your wonderful boys, aren't they all scrumptious? – hello, my darling, Mummy's here – oh, goodness, is that your cleanest jersey? Well, I expect Matron can do something about that, she's such a dear, isn't she, Mr Victor, I'm sure you're so glad to have her...'

The arrival of a parent at school was at any time a shameful event discouraged by the boys however much they longed for tuck. Of course at the beginning and end of term it could hardly be avoided – indeed in the latter case was to be welcome provided the parent limited its role to trunk-handling and did not dawdle about trying to talk to Mr Victor or to read exam results on notice boards. One mother – to the eternal shame of her son – had even gone angrily through the changing room lockers in search of a missing football sock. But at other and unsolicited times parents were not welcome. If the cry went up 'So-and-so, your mother's here' So-and-so would scamper off, eager both to prevent the parent from straying any distance from the car and to lay hold on the tuck – perhaps a birthday cake – which would undoubtedly accompany the visitor. Chatting in low tones through the car window for a few minutes – no risk of any passing fellow overhearing any parental gaffe – then scampering off to Matron with the goodies was the best outcome of such a visit. Home was one thing and school another: it was not well to mix the two.

Young Marvell was not in the least perturbed by his mother's attention, however. Endearments and physical displays of affection that would have had the average boy cringing and blushing to the roots passed without impression over his equable demeanour.

'My darling, I can tell you're wonderfully happy and I'm sure everyone's looking after you beautifully – hello, Mrs Victor, no tea for me, dear, thank you – I really hoped we might walk in the grounds as a matter of fact, Mr Victor, just the two of us – I've got a particular reason – goodness! doesn't that sound mysterious? – I'll explain instantly – Max, darling (for thus her little son was, incredibly, named) don't fly away, I'll be back soon.'

Mr Victor's returning suspicions at the strange request – fine though the day was – for a private outdoor interview were soon allayed by the enthusiasm with which Mrs Maxwell admired the grounds, Mr Victor steering her away from the collapsed Hut. Not that it was possible entirely to avoid evidence of it since – just as village people used to pillage the remains of the local abandoned monastery for building materials, carrying off chunks of free, ready-dressed stone for their own purposes – so the boys of The Dell were avidly cannibalising the Hut for planks and timbers towards the construction of their tree-houses and camps in the wood. While the materials of the Hut might have contributed to the wealth of Mr Bolton's no longer secret store, the work of separating, sorting and carting were too much for him and, having removed a few handsome metal bolts, he left the ruins to the juvenile predators who could be seen in every direction hefting timber.

'Such gorgeous grounds, Mr Victor, really the boys are so lucky – all these acres to play in – all that lovely wood for them to make things with – all that lovely long grass – which reminds me of what I wanted to say...'

And she told him about the pony. Young Max had, it seemed, been given a pony for his birthday – a very small one befitting his size, of course, but a real pony that had actually cost a lot of money and needed a fair amount of looking after. But the looking after wasn't the main thing, Mrs Marvell said –

the livery stables took care of that – it was the loving. Although the animal had only arrived during the Easter holidays it and Max had formed an instant bond of devoted friendship and now Flop – for thus had the creature been named – Flop was pining. Pining. How would it be now – she was sure Mr Victor would be sympathetic – if Flop came and stayed at The Dell? There was grass for him to crop, Max and the other children to look after him – he would be no trouble at all in fact and there was barely a month of term to go.

All Mr Victor's personal and pedagogic instincts were in revolt at this idea. It was novel, it was proposed by a parent, it involved a change in the routine of the school and it smacked of individual pleasure rather than team commitment. But the 'Well, I really don't think...' stalled in his throat as will happen when commercial considerations barge in on the bold stance of a man of principle. It was not just the 'Of course, we'll pay for his keep – he costs the earth at livery' that stopped him but rather the thought that if her son's involvement in the Blackstone business should ever become known it would be as well that his mother should feel warmly towards the establishment that had unwittingly harboured her son's corrupter.

Anyway Mr Victor knew nothing whatever of horses, though he would like it to be supposed that he had such knowledge as befitted every middle-class Englishman as part of his birthright and upbringing. Naturally the motor car was a twentieth century abomination (though he was obliged, proudly ignorant albeit of its workings, to drive one himself) and the horse was God's chosen means of transport for man, but the fact remained that Mr Victor had no basis of knowledge from which to argue against the introduction of such an animal and his feeble 'What about a stable?' was waved aside with a gay dismissive laugh at the idea of a pony requiring a stable in mid-summer. And as for tack and fodder Mrs Maxwell could see there were plenty of outhouses and such-like where that could be kept – she waved imprecisely in the direction of a small dilapidated brick building that had perhaps once contained the house's original heating boiler and of a glassless greenhouse that Mr Victor had hoped she would not notice.

And that was that. Mrs Victor might not be very pleased, suspicious as she always was of the sort of feminine charm of a Mrs Marvell and of its effect on her husband, but really Mrs Marvell was hard to resist: the confidence born of money, beauty and a compliant husband was overwhelming. Returned to the house, Mr Victor detected a certain buzz about the place, the cause of which he did not ascertain until after Mrs Marvell's departure which she took, again declining tea and pausing only to say that there were some charming friends she so wanted him to meet who had a delightful boy – Mr Victor suddenly all attention – before hurrying away to make arrangements for the transport of Flop. Then Mrs Victor met him with 'You must come and meet our new matron.' And when he did he realised what the buzz had been about, for the new matron, Gay Phelps, was an absolute corker and Mr Victor, on the wings, as it were, of Mrs Marvell's charm, went up to her and, though he had not seen her since she was a little girl, kissed her on her peach-like cheek.

❊ CHAPTER XVI ❊

It was the last kiss Gay was to receive at The Dell. Not because no one else wished to implant one – on the contrary, within a day of her arrival every member of the school would have given a week's sweet allowance for the pleasure – but because Gay was of the degree of beauty so outside the ordinary that no one dared approach. Mr Victor's welcoming kiss had been an avuncular privilege, Gay being the daughter of an old friend who ran an establishment similar to The Dell in another part of the country. Gay was a beauty beyond mortal reach: naturally blonde with straight flowing hair, perfect regular features, a soft and immaculate complexion.

Just as Mrs Marvell, with her flamboyant dress sense and pungent perfume, brought an aura of affluence to the austere environment of The Dell so Gay brought beauty to its plainness, and unlike Mrs Marvell she was not a passing vision but a perpetual presence. There she was brightly in the dormitory every morning to make the day welcome; there she was at the head of the breakfast table to ladle the porridge, there at lunch and supper; there – wonderfully – at bed-time to wash hair, clip nails and, if you were lucky, tuck you up. For Gay was not only beautiful, she was loving; not only loving but hard-working and efficient, compassionate and carefree.

Her conquest of The Dell was instant and total. There was surely a lightness in Mr Victor's step – even Mrs Victor realised quickly how little she had to fear, for Gay, though highly attractive, was not in the least coquettish and kept constant male attention at appropriate distance without froideur or tease. There was hardly a boy who did not warm to her. Finally, there were two whose hearts were set alight with unusual blaze – our hero and Mr Denman.

Although barely five years older than him Gay seemed to Johnny hopelessly out of his star. No more inaccessible and worshipful seemed the high-turreted lady of eleventh century Languedoc to her heart-enslaved knight than did Gay to Johnny. For him she transformed not just the rewardless drudgery and restraints of school but introduced into his life a meaning and a purpose which had been absent, of whose possible existence indeed he had been unaware. She became his planet round which he orbited in magnetic slavery, wholly devoted to her and the love that blazed in him.

Mr Denman, meanwhile, ten years her senior rather than five her junior, was similarly struck. In a state, as has been mentioned, of torpor ever since the Hut-collapse episode – a state verging at times, particularly in class, on the catatonic – Mr Denman was stunned anew by Gay's arrival and beauty. Mooning about, staring and loitering in her vicinity was the character of his initial reaction to her.

Amongst the boys Johnny was in a distinctly privileged position – by his age, by his role as Captain of School and now as virtual member of staff. This position he exploited to the full. It was, for example, one of the usually less welcome roles of the school prefects to help matron at bed-time, particularly with the youngsters. As an alternative to mucking about in the woods it had never appealed and the former matron really too capable and experienced to require such assistance. But with Gay it was different. The prefects as a body rallied to her support and from the moment the first seven-year-old was due up in dormitory there would be the faithful band, reporting for duty. No task however small was beneath their office: just to squeeze out and hang up a neglected flannel was an act of loving joy if by it the agent might save Matron the least labour. It was not so much, however, a scramble for her approval or vying for her attention that motivated them to such acts as a passionate commitment to duty born of love, for there are in truth fewer passions stronger in the human heart than the passion of loving service.

'Is this what you're looking for, Matron?' 'Come on out of the bathroom, Bell, can't you see Matron wants to slosh out ?' 'Lights are off in Coldstream, Matron.' 'Shall I do prayers in Grenadiers, Matron?' 'Was that talking in Scots I heard? Tell them to shut up, Beeston, will you – Matron's got enough on her hands.' And so on, an unending buzz of loving busy-ness through which the star herself moved with a dignity and calm that spread about her a radiance and an atmosphere of contented devotion that closed tired eyelids without a qualm and set troubled hearts at rest.

And when that was over the prefects, their own (unsupervised) bed-time approaching, would go down to the pantry for slices of bread and dripping that was their material reward. And there for a short while the Captain of School might enjoy the wonder of a few minutes alone with Gay – at which point a conversational paralysis would come over him as her beauty and the wonder of her presence invaded his heart afresh.

Imagine then Johnny's excitement when at breakfast one morning Mr Victor said 'By the way, Clarke, Miss Phelps will be joining you for your English lessons with 4B – help you out a bit.' For Gay was not a real matron, Mr Victor explained, in fact she was going to train to be a teacher and she had come to The Dell for general experience. French, alas, she was not qualified to cover but anyone could teach English. As a matter of educational theory the concept of 'team teaching' was yet to be born and would as progressive theory have been abhorrent nonsense to Mr Victor; as a matter of practicality, however, there was something to be said for two young people pooling their inexperience and floundering together.

So it was that *Toad of Toad Hall* had two people to direct it.

And of course the impact of this new arrangement on 4B was electric. Clamorous enough had been the reading sessions under Johnny's tutelage; deafening and chaotic were they now as, for example, one member of the form appealed to Matron for promotion from the general run of ferrets etc. to a more distinguished role while Johnny – who had passed over that same young person for that very role for disorderly conduct – was busy in another corner of the room. It was as well that 4B's classroom was somewhat out of the way or the din might have attracted Mr Victor's censorious attention earlier and who knows how that might not have scotched a turn of events that was to develop so gloriously?

For 4B's classroom was really a stable. Gestures of conversion to classroom had been few: that is to say, chairs and desks had been installed and a blackboard with its easel. The floor was rough concrete, sloping gently for obvious reasons of animal sanitation to a wide shallow gutter at one end. There were no windows so it was just as well that it had only three brick walls, the fourth consisting in its entirety of the conventional stable door – that is, a double door separated at shoulder height. This in the summer could be thrown partly or wholly open, giving the room an airy lightness that was delectable and much in contrast with the freezing gloom that characterised it in winter when the sparrows who nested in its rafters and whose cheepings constituted a continuous background to study were obliged to come in and out through the gap between the wall and the corrugated asbestos of the roof.

Giving on to the playing fields and grounds, the classroom almost merged with that outdoors that was the boys' natural summer habitat. Grasshoppers found their way in and though their capture and detention inside a desk might create a momentary diversion they were too numerous not to become regular and unremarked visitors; ditto the butterflies and wasps that if they found their way into conventional classrooms would create serious interruptions with flappings and openings of windows; a kestrel, hovering above the long grass at the far side of the cricket field could be appreciated by all at once at a mere swivel in the chair; similarly a furry caterpillar, as big and brown as a chippolata, though remarkable, was gently left to make its crinkling way up the wall without interference.

In such an environment with so thin a division between indoors and out it was not surprising that the reading of a play that is set in the open should soon spill outdoors. And spill it did. Nor surprising that once spilled a play-reading imperceptibly became a book-in-hand production.

'Are you going to be a part, Matron, Miss Phelps?'

'She can be the barge-woman.'

'Or Mama Rabbit.'

'Don't be a clot, those are horrible, weedy parts. She must be Phoebe.'

'Why don't we do Snow White and the Seven Dwarves, then Miss Phelps can be Snow White?'

'Yes, and Clarke can be the Wicked Witch.'

'Bags I be Dopey!'

'Fainz I be Sneezy.'

'Ferguson can be Sneezy – he's always got hay-fever.'

'That's right, always sneezing and wiping your nose and blubbing, aren't you, Ferguson?'

'You're such a wet, Ferguson.'

Johnny's magisterial 'Shut up and sit down' was less effectual than usual since the above conversation was conducted while straggling across the cricket field to the rough grassy mound beyond. But Gay's delighted exclamation of 'This is it!' brought all to silence and attention. 'This is it – this is the riverbank where Marigold lies at the very beginning and then the animals all come on.'

'Who's Marigold?'

'She's that wet bit at the start and the end. We're not doing that bit, Miss Phelps.'

'Matron could be Marigold, you know.'

'All right then, everyone, sit down,' Johnny now commanded. 'Let's start. Matron, will you do the Marigold bit?'

' "Hello, is that the Exchange? I want River Bank 1001... Hello, is that the Water Rat's house...?" '

And so they got under way. The 'wet bit' was instantaneously transformed by Matron's entrancing tones and there was even hot competition for the previously despised part of Nurse since that involved dialogue with Marigold.

'Gosh, is that the bell already?'

'Boring old cricket!'

'Can we come back after tea, Matron, and carry on?'

'All right, for half an hour, before junior bed-time.'

And so there they were again later that afternoon, though one or two forgetful Wild Wooders had to be found in the real woods where they had reverted to camp-building. This rehearsal taking place during free time those unlucky enough not to be in 4B – formerly the most despised, now the most envied, class in the school – hung about in the vicinity of the river bank hoping if not for inclusion in the cast at least to be able to hear and see Matron in her new role. Mr Denman, turning out at about that time for an evening stint of grass-mowing, let his machine stand idle and loitered too.

But it was soon junior bed-time and they had to disperse.

'You know what, Johnny,' Gay confided to her fellow teacher that evening over their after-duty cocoa and bread-and-dripping. 'We really could do a proper production of *Toad of Toad Hall*, you know.'

'You mean, really act it? – with costumes and everything?'

'Why not? I could make the costumes. I'm sure Mrs Logsdon would help too.'

'It couldn't just be 4B, though, could it? There aren't enough of them.'

'True, we'd have to bring in other people.'

'We'd need a caravan,' said Johnny dubiously.

'Perhaps Mr Denman could make one.'

Crikey, thought Johnny, this girl was something: had she any idea how much it had taken out of the man to build a small bridge out of hardboard? A caravan!

'Where would we do it now the Hut's fallen down?' he queried, his excitement rising in spite of himself.

'Outside, of course, where we have it at the moment. People could sit on rugs and watch – there's changing room under the trees.'

'As long as it doesn't rain.'

'As long as it doesn't rain.'

They jolly well could do it. Of course it wouldn't be nearly as good as *The Mikado* and they only had four weeks or so in which to rehearse and all that but it would be better than nothing and help the term to end with a bit of a bang. The idea kept Johnny awake that night as the midsummer day so slowly dimmed behind the curtains. How wonderful to be with Gay practically all day – that's what it would mean. And he pictured her lying on the grass in a pink frock talking on her daffodil telephone: 'May I really come one day? How lovely...' It was an image to go to sleep with. Marigold, Marigold.

❋ CHAPTER XVII ❋

And then Flop arrived. Mrs Marvell had lost no time in off-loading this additional burden to her domestic responsibilities. Within two days of her request Flop was securely tethered to a stake planted deep upon the very spot on which she had made that request, and contentedly munching the long grass.

The arrival of a large horse-box drew considerable attention and onlookers were amazed to see so huge a vehicle contain so small an animal. It seemed scarcely bigger than a labrador, it was almost completely round and it had the family trait – though to somewhat less a degree – of red hair, a large hank of which flopped – hence perhaps its name – over its big brown eyes. Obviously, in choosing an animal for her little boy, Mrs Marvell had had to consider his tenderness, his diminutive size and his complete absence of experience or evidence of aptitude. Flop had been sold to her as safe and very suitable for a beginner. Safe he certainly showed every sign of being, manifesting not the slightest interest in any aspect of his environment except the grass and being quite impervious to stimulus.

The involuntary 'Oohs' and 'Aahs' and even 'Isn't he sweets?' barely outlasted first impressions when his stolidity and – in the matter of getting him out of the horse-box – downright obstinacy were at once evident. A substantial quantity of brand-new tack accompanied this little Shetland and that had to be stored in an outhouse. Mrs Marvell was not in the horse-box party herself so it was not clear, as the animal took up residence, who was responsible for it and its belongings. Obviously such matters as saddles, bits and bridles were quite beyond its owner. But here too the new star came to the rescue. Gay Phelps was scarcely out of the pony phase herself. Within hours of its arrival it was saddled and Marvell – properly attired in jodhpurs and an enormous hard hat – was on horseback being led round the field by Matron. Free rides were then the order of the day until Flop, barely compliant at the outset, refused to take another step.

And so a further novel element was added to life at The Dell.

And it wasn't the last in what Johnny began to realise was the most extraordinary term of his life. He was Head Boy, he had won an exhibition to public school; he had come out on top in a unique finale to Sports Day, a day made all the more historic to the school as a whole by the collapse of the Hut; Mr Blackstone had disappeared for reasons, it was given out, of sudden ill-health; he had as good as become a member of staff himself; Matron had burst upon his heart with all her beauty – they were doing outdoor plays and there was a horse too. And now here was another novelty: Singer Samuel.

At her last visit Mrs Marvell had mentioned some 'charming people' who had a son. Of course, Mr Victor, scenting a fee, had taken note but given little further thought to the matter: Mrs Marvell was an impulsive and talkative person who would be just as likely to forget all about it as do anything. But the following exeat Sunday she had turned up with these 'charming people' and introduced them to Mr and Mrs Victor with 'I know you'll love one another'. To Mr Victor's astonishment – though it went quite without remark by Mrs Marvell – Mr and Mrs Samuel came from the USA. If any race or nation represented to Mr Victor the hated image of modernity it was the American. They were loud, they were unrestrained in their social manners, calling people by their first names within moments of introduction; they were optimistic and successful;

they were rich; they had no deference towards the land of their origin; they took all the credit for winning the war and they did murderous things to the English language with every utterance. It was also well known that their children were insolent to their parents and grossly indulged. Must he really accept into the school a spoilt and cheeky little American boy?

A few moments of talk, however, swept aside at least the virulence of Mr Victor's prejudices even if not the prejudices themselves which slunk back to their lairs like temporarily disappointed hounds. For Mr and Mrs Samuel were actually modest, and young Singer – how typical, though, of the Americans that with a Christian name for a surname a boy should be given a surname for a Christian name – Singer was polite and attentive, addressing Mr Victor unfailingly as 'sir' throughout, except when he called him Mr Victor, which was however slightly disconcerting in one so young.

Mr and Mrs Samuel – and good heavens they must be Jewish as well! – instantly wrapped everyone and everything at The Dell in the same gorgeous material as did Mrs Marvell. 'It's a fine place you've got here, Mr Victor,' was uttered almost on alighting from the car and nothing was seen that did not elicit favourable comment: even the frayed red blankets with which the beds were uniformly spread were pronounced 'bright'. Every boy encountered was quizzed in the most personal but inoffensive manner and pronounced 'charming' or 'cute'.

For Mr Victor never had a sale been so swimmingly effected. Mr Samuel was in England for eighteen months or so – he was in the 'entertainments industry', as he termed it, so naturally Mr Victor, echoes of 'Hollywood' reverberating uncomfortably in his mind, enquired no further – and he wished to place his son in an English boarding school without delay. Indeed barely had the cheque been banked – now Mr Victor could pay for the hideously costly repair of the lawn-mower – when Singer was fully installed as a member of the school.

If Mr Victor had been possessed of certain prejudices regarding Americans so too were the boys. It was at first something of a surprise to them that Mrs Samuel did not call her husband 'Elmer' and that he did not smoke a cigar; further that their son did not have a crew-cut, did not chew gum, was not called 'Junior' and did not say 'Gee'. He was, however, almost as much of a novelty – though of course on quite different grounds – as Gay and for a while the school was abuzz about him.

There was first of all the matter of uniform. Uniform at The Dell was almost entirely grey – socks, trousers, shirts, pullovers. Its distinctive colour was dull gold with which the otherwise grey ties were striped, as were the V's of the more expensive kind of pullover. The greyness made – as it was partly intended to do – for cheapness and ease of purchase. Most items of uniform could be bought in local shops, Mrs Victor keeping a stock of the more distinctive articles like caps secondhand so that several garments currently being worn were originally the property of people now old enough to have children in the school. From this store had Johnny been kitted out throughout his time at The Dell, even down to that first pair of long trousers that were his prerogative as Head of School.

The astonishing thing about the contents of Singer's trunk was that they were all brand new – as was also the trunk itself, his name beautifully stencilled on its lid in shiny black paint. And it wasn't only the special items like the ties, the cap and the pullovers that parents often found they were obliged or wished to buy new, but even the vests and pants and handkerchiefs (12). Clearly Mrs Samuel, anxious to do the right thing for her boy in this strange land, had actually visited the not very grand department store in Kensington that, combining inconveniently low stocks with extremely high prices , enjoyed the franchise on uniform for The Dell, as for many other schools. Johnny looked on in wonder as Matron unpacked this treasure – each item had also been expertly marked, including the stamping of the initials in little brass nail-heads on the underside of the shoes' insteps. Singer was seemingly indifferent to the enviable wealth of which he was uniquely possessed.

'Hey, John, can you tell me how to do this darned thing?'

To Johnny's amazement Singer was referring to the school tie which he was experimentally crossing round his neck. He had never, it seemed, worn one. Remembering the lessons he had himself received in the process by his father at home lest he be shamed and thereby rendered vulnerable by his ignorance at school, Johnny smiled and helped. Singer evinced no embarrassment at what should have been a gross humiliation, thanked Johnny after a demonstration or two with 'I guess I got it now' and turned to other matters.

So easy an acquisition of local lore was characteristic of Singer's adaptation to life at The Dell. He put his foot wrong frequently but never gave offence. One day Johnny encountered him coming down the main staircase.

'I say, Singer, you're not allowed down here.'

'That so? Why not?' from Singer. It was not a challenge, merely a query.

'Well, it's... well, actually it's reserved for staff and the Head Boy.'

'Oh, I see. Kind of a privilege, huh?' (He was proud to have grasped this alien concept) 'I'm sorry, John, I didn't know. I'll go down the other stairs. I'm sorry Mr Denman, sir.' (passing at that moment). And his apology had no underlying note of huffiness about it – it was a straightforward, ingenuous apology.

His complete ignorance of such fundamental matters as the rules of cricket, his slowness to respond to hierarchical principles and to the whole concept of punishment rendered him dangerously laughable, but his willingness to learn and to fit in and contribute was blatant and irrepressible so that he was an instant favourite.

Certainly with Johnny. Although a year or more divided them Singer addressed Johnny with an ease that from anyone else in the year group might have been judged cheeky or sucking up. His use of the correct name 'John' was presumptuous but irresistible and Johnny warmed to his warmth.

'Mr Victor seems a pretty nice guy,' he opined one day soon after his arrival. To Johnny it was astonishing to refer to the headmaster as a 'guy', as if he were a human being like anyone else and to pass a personal judgment on him. Indeed Singer's ease of manner made no distinction of persons and he would be as loquacious and at ease in the company of Mr Victor – company not normally sought by the boys – as with anyone else.

'I guess that takes a pretty good eye, sir,' he remarked once during the regular mystery of ruling the creases at which Mr Victor was an awesome practitioner. It required the assistance of several acolytes who stood about with measuring tapes or string or nothing at all but their readiness to respond to Mr Victor's need in this arcane process. To talk at all at such a time was to risk an ill-tempered retort since Mr Victor brought to the job equal quantities of concentration and irritability. But Singer got away with it. 'Comes with practice, I guess,' he went on, oblivious, while those around him tensed in anticipation, of the bark if not bite he was likely to provoke by his remarks. 'You musta done an awful lot of these in your time, Mr Victor, sir. By the way, exactly how long is a cricket pitch?'

'Twenty two yards,' an acolyte quickly and quietly responded, hoping to shut him up and to head off Mr Victor's impatient retort.

'Really? Now why was it that length, I wonder? I wanna know everything about cricket,' he confided warmly.

While the acolytes shrank in renewed apprehension of a blast Mr Victor calmly answered his question, the boys having failed to allow for his love of the game and willingness to talk about it, particularly if by so doing he could reveal his own extensive knowledge in contrast with his interlocutor's extensive ignorance. Hunched and concentrated on his task though he was, Mr Victor, steering his venerable machine which marked the white lines with practised aplomb, responded to Singer's unique enquiry with detailed fact embellished with historical anecdote. He became quite expansive as he talked, relaxed somewhat, made the odd gesticulation and, though continuing with the task in hand with equal accuracy, did so with an increasing flourish as Singer hung on his every word.

The acolytes slowly relaxed in astonishment as Mr Victor talked on and Singer listened. But their anxiety instantly returned when Singer suddenly announced 'Well, I must go and join John for his rehearsal now, if you'll excuse me. Thank you, sir. I will look forward to hearing more some other time.'

Mr Victor seemed uncharacteristically non-plussed: for one thing nobody excused themselves from Mr Victor in any situation : they awaited dismissal and for another...

' 'John'? What 'rehearsal'? ' He looked up in enquiry.

'I'm sure one of these guys will explain, sir. I told John five and I don't want to be late.'

Mr Victor returned to his former hunched position with the line-marker on Singer's departure as one of the acolytes hesitantly explained about Johnny and Gay and *Toad of Toad Hall*. He made no comment and the usual glum atmosphere returned as the cheerful figure of Singer Samuel was seen disappearing in the direction of the River Bank.

❊ CHAPTER XVIII ❊

Little that came from the kitchens at The Dell was relished, though Mrs Bolton, the cook, was a pleasant contrast to her disagreeable husband, the gardener. While tuck was of supreme importance the standard fare was eatable but not delectable. In fact the only item that excited any appetite was the dog's biscuits. These were stored in a bag on an open shelf near the door and were thus subject to occasional daring raids, the kitchen being, of course, out of bounds. The biscuits came – like fruit pastilles – in a variety of unnatural colours such as violent yellow, raspberry pink and black, and opinions varied as to their relative merits, some even claiming that they actually all tasted the same, regardless of hue. The most popular, however, were the black, perhaps by analogy with the black pastilles, the blackcurrant flavour. They were not, of course, to everybody's taste.

There was always a cooked dish for breakfast, after the porridge. On Sunday there were, in accordance with English custom, boiled eggs. Boiling some fifty eggs for three and a half minutes was a challenge beyond Mrs Bolton's powers. It was alleged that once she'd got the great pan seething nicely she immersed the eggs in the boiling water singly and extracted them singly; the immersion procedure was immediately followed by the extraction procedure but without regard – as how could it not be since eggs are not readily distinguishable one from another? – without regard to how long they had been in the pan. Thus some eggs spent several minutes in the boiling water, others only a few seconds. So it was a matter of chance as to whether one's allotted egg was hard-boiled or virtually raw, or anything in between, and this occasioned much lively anticipation at the breakfast table.

'Can I have that small one, sir?' – this request in the hope that the smaller the egg the more likely it would be to be cooked and therefore to have none of the uncooked white, the diaphanous slime, that was the boys' principal horror.

'Get what you're given, Graves.'

'Yes, sir.'

'And like it.'

'Yes, sir.'

'Bet mine'll be a real bouncer.'

'Last week I couldn't get my spoon into mine.'

'I couldn't get my *knife* into mine.'

'Swank!'

'Thank you, sir. Gosh, mine looks about done right. Miracle. You did say I could have your crusts, didn't you, sir?' – (another distinctive feature of Sunday breakfast being that the staff got toast instead of bread).

'I thought it was Thompson's turn.'

'Oh no, sir. Thompson had them last week – didn't you, Tommy?'

'I don't know that I can quite remember whether I did or not.'

'Oh you fibber! You cheat! You…'

'Shut up, Graves, or I'll eat them myself.'

'Yes, sir.'

'Sir, I'm not sure my egg's… quite right, if you know what I mean, sir.'

'I don't, Barnes.'

'Well, sir, I mean it's sort of cooked all right, I suppose, but it's kind of greenish in the white bits.'

Lively interest in Barnes' egg now shown by neighbours.

Muttered grumbles about the condition of the eggs were the order of the day but there was something about this carefully phrased remonstration on the part of the normally meek Barnes that held some unusual promise.

'Gosh, it does, sir. Barnes is right – it looks like' – and the naughty word had to be whispered – 'snot.'

'Cor! And it pongs too. Whiff that, Tommy!'

'Wow!'

Word spread rapidly down the table. 'Barnes has got a whiffy egg – smells like a stink bomb.'

'It's green like phlegm too. I wonder if he'll have to eat it.'

'Give it here, Barnes,' Mr Denman commanded. Applying it to his nose cursorily, the customary response 'It's perfectly all right' ready on his lips, Mr Denman, all eyes avidly upon him, withdrew it with unpremeditated promptness but without evincing any more overt reaction and without comment. He then intensified the drama by taking it over to Mrs Victor for professional evaluation. Mrs Victor's practised eye quickly identified the egg as bad, or so it was to be inferred as, instead of it being returned to Barnes with the hearty injunction that it was perfectly good and that he should eat it, it was discreetly carried away, not to be mentioned again.

A hush then prevailed in Barnes' vicinity as if some small unexpected victory had been won but must not be gloated over.

'You can have my crusts, Barnes, as you haven't got an egg,' kindly offered Mr Denman.

'Gosh, thank you, sir' – and the treasured off-cuts were reverentially passed down to him.

'Oh, sir, that's a swizz. You said *I* could have them this Sunday.'

'Shut up, Graves, you can see what's happened.'

'Yes, sir.'

After bed-making and inspection came letter-writing. This activity was to Johnny an otiose one since, his father being the local rector and the school attending Matins at the parish church, he saw his parents every Sunday. Even more was it a redundant activity for all the boys on this particular Sunday, it being an exeat – or 'exeant', as Mr Victor expressed it generally, 'exeatis' if addressing the boys and – if he were giving permission (rare, this) for a boy to be out of school for some respectable reason like a family funeral – 'exeas', a word which always sent the supplicant away smiling.

The logic of writing at ten o'clock a letter to parents whom one would see in person at twelve o'clock was questionable but there was no one to question it. Had any justification been required Mr Victor would have offered something on these lines: Letter-writing was an ancient art to be preserved against the cultural depredations of the telephone; a weekly report gave fulness to the record of their sons' time at The Dell that parents no doubt stored with care. That it also kept the boys quiet and their Sunday best clean during that awkward hour between breakfast and Matins was undoubtedly part of the hidden agenda. Besides, it was no great hardship: why, he himself had in similar circumstances been obliged to translate the day's Collect into Latin.

So fifty-three boys were sat at their desks, fifty-two eggs of varying culinary readiness working their way through fifty-two digestive tracts. Requests for tuck – indeed requests for anything – being forbidden in letters home, the boys were reduced to lifelessly recording such items of news as that the school had defeated Folly Grove by twenty three runs in the previous day's match, that Marvell's pony had joined the school, as had Miss Phelps, 'the super new matron'. Johnny was to add with some pride – a pride he was later that day to regret – that she and he were working together to put on a performance of *Toad of Toad Hall*. Some were moved to mention the episode of Barnes' egg but this was later censored. In order to save on stationery no envelopes were provided for those whose letters were to be delivered by hand, these letters being put in the inside pockets of the suits worn only on Sundays and for away matches.

Caps on, the boys walked in crocodile to church, on entry to which – that is, at the last possible moment – they were each issued with a penny for the collection. These pennies – the only money the boys ever handled and then for just a short time before giving it away to an unknown cause – generated some interest in what was otherwise a wholly familiar place and an entirely predictable proceeding. Dates were compared – 'Gosh! mine's Queen Victoria – look!'; futile attempts at spit-and-polishing were made, coins were spun, swapped, rolled, accidentally dropped, put in pockets (but could you remember which one?) before the master-on-duty, in a barely reverential hiss, put a stop to it.

And so, while the devices and desires of their own hearts were duly lamented and the noble army of martyrs crossed the liturgical stage, the boys engaged in pleasurable anticipation of lunch at home. For Johnny, the fact that his father was presiding and was, even now, ascending the pulpit steps was a matter of no moment. Although some of his contemporaries expressed sympathy at his having to go to church even in the holidays he found it no hardship: it was simply what he did and the way things were. Not that he had, so far as he could detect, any strong religious feelings, but on this occasion – instead of eyeing old Major Cordingley in the front row to see how long it would be before he groaned quietly, as was his wont, and nodded off – he found himself contemplating the phrase 'world without end'.

Familiar enough, it was. Like 'Amen'. But what did it mean exactly? Did it mean end in time or end in space? Did it mean that the world was never going to come to an end or that it was without limits? – that all the years of history so far were as nothing compared to what was going to happen, in which case we obviously weren't all going to kill each other and blow up the world with H-bombs – but then where would everybody go? I mean, it's a well known fact that the population is growing all the time, what with diseases being cured and so on. Well, perhaps they'd have to go to other planets, like in Dan Dare, travel trillions of miles in spaceships to places like Mars and live there – if there was the kind of stuff you could live on and people like the Mekon would let you.

Then if you take 'world' to mean not planet Earth but the whole blooming universe then what the phrase meant was that the universe just went on and on to outer space where it might be too cold to live or you got completely sizzled by the sun or bombarded by meteorites. The trouble was that 'without end' just didn't apply in life: even one of Mr Victor's Latin lessons came to an end – ha ha – and even his own time at The Dell would be ending in a few weeks.

'In the name of the Father, and of the Son and the Holy Ghost...' – at any rate his father was coming to an end. Of course he might ask him about it – he was supposed to understand these things.

Sunday being the day of work for Johnny's father, the traditional roast was normally eaten on Saturday; an exception was made on exeat Sunday, so that Johnny should not miss this weekly treat. A Sunday roast was regularly served at The Dell but fifty-three helpings off one joint, leaving sufficient over for cold meat the following day, made for only modest helpings: Mrs Victor had become adept at carving beef wafer thin, which may have accorded with gourmet convention where beef was concerned but was no good to the boys who wanted quantity. At home, by contrast, there was not only more but also some choice – although that would normally extend no further than well done or not so well done. On this particular occasion, however, there was something of a special treat.

'Gosh, chicken!' exclaimed Johnny as his mother brought in the rare fowl and set it down in front of her husband for carving.

'Well, it's a celebration,' said his father, eyeing the bird proudly and ostentatiously turning it around – he had not yet given up hoping that his wife would one day understand that a bird was carved with its legs pointing away from the carver.

'Your exhibition,' explained his mother, removing her apron and draping it discreetly around her husband's waist to protect his clerical grey as he wielded the carving knife and fork.

Johnny tried to feel proud. He realised he wasn't very good at feeling proud. Did they know what mark he'd got in Maths?

'Now what kind of meat would you like?' enquired his father, slicing assiduously. 'There's a lovely drumstick.'

'Drumstick, please,' said Johnny, thus prompted, and silently hankering for bits without bones but not daring to ask.

'Now,' said his father, the carving done and everyone tucking in, 'let's see,' and he turned to Johnny's letter of that morning that was beside his place, like an agenda.

Nothing had at any time been said about Mr Blackstone and his precipitate departure even though his father had been at least close to if not involved in the action on that fateful Sports Day, but Johnny had said that he was now doing a lot of French teaching.

'As in the old days,' said his father, 'when the older children taught the younger. Oh, and *Toad of Toad Hall*, eh? That sounds fun. So this Miss Phelps, the new matron...' – and Johnny suddenly found, like a man whose handhold has unexpectedly and irretrievably given way on the precipitous mountain side, that he was plunging helplessly into a horrifying condition of extreme self-consciousness, that the blood was surging up into his face in an irrepressible scarlet flood and he clenched his teeth, looking down at his plate, in a desperate attempt to keep it at bay. 'Was that the pretty blonde girl at the end of the junior row in church this morning?' pursued his father, innocently merciless.

'Yes, she's...' Johnny frowned at his gravy, willing his blush to subside. He knew not how to continue. 'Beautiful'; 'smashing'; 'I love her.' What! What?!

Johnny was too old now to be read to, too old to sit with his mother on the drawing room window-seat looking at religious picture books; he even felt too old to bury himself in the high-backed and -sided porter's chair in the hall with *Swallows and Amazons*. So he mooched about. It was hard, anyway, to get down to anything on an exeat Sunday – by the time you'd got the toys out and a game going it was time to put them away.

You didn't even change out of school uniform.

At tea he began to feel restive. Instead of the usual feeling, as the sun dipped towards 'going back to school', of his heart dipping with it, Johnny recognised a quite new feeling: he wanted to get back to school. It must be, he supposed, because all his real worries were over – it wasn't long before the end of term, he'd done his work and got his award and all really he'd got to think about was *Toad of Toad Hall*. And Miss Phelps. Gay. Matron. That was it, and he was free now, strolling round the sunny summer garden, to reflect cautiously on that terrifying bout of blushing that had beset him against his will at lunch. In truth he was day-dreaming about lying in the long grass with her, planning the play, talking and imagining. He wanted to be back at school – now, where she was. He'd have wanted to be in the middle of the Sahara without a drop of water if that's where she had been.

Not, sadly, that she'd be at Evensong, he realised, because she'd be putting the juniors to bed. Evensong in the Victors' drawing room with Mrs Victor at the piano was for the seniors only. 'The day thou gavest Lord is ended / The darkness falls at thy behest,' they'd sing, the words wafting out over the wistaria into the light long evening. The first bell would ring outside. Johnny would read the lesson. During prayers he would listen for the sounds of the juniors going to bed. 'Matron, can I go downstairs to get my book?' a little voice would ask. 'Of course you can, Monkton,' would come the sweet reply. 'But don't be late.' 'And no talking on the way there or back' – a harsher tone, Beeston, probably, who'd wangled getting off Evensong to be on duty. Lucky pig.

'Dad,' Johnny asked, 'do you happen to have a copy of *Toad of Toad Hall* by any chance?'

Later that evening Johnny was on duty in the bathroom. He'd seen Beeston off: 'OK, Bees, I'll take over,' he had said. 'But, Clarke…' 'It's all right – I'll do it,' Johnny smartly interrupted as if he were nobly doing Beeston a favour – which in normal circumstances he would have been.

'It seems a pity the blackbirds should get all the cherries,' remarked Gay during a lull in the proceedings.

'Cherries?'

'Yes, look,' she said, pointing out of the window, and as she turned her head the evening sun glinted on her golden hair.

Of course Johnny knew perfectly well – everybody did – that in a corner of the kitchen yard there grew a very large cherry tree. And of course everyone knew that some years it had cherries – little reddish-yellow things that didn't look up to much and which the blackbirds generally had before anyone could think whether it was worth the climb to harvest them.

'Are they... quite tasty?'

'Of course they are.' Gay waved a junior boy's damp flannel playfully in his face. 'Just because they're not big and dark red like those vulgar Mediterranean things. My uncle grows them in Kent.'

'It's certainly a big crop,' said Johnny. 'Never seen so many. Oh, Mrs Victor' – the headmaster's wife had just come in – ' do you think we could pick the cherries?' He indicated out of the window.

Permission (surprisingly) granted, volunteers appeared instantly from nowhere. Deferring bed-time – even the thirteen-year-olds were in bed by eight on the longest of summer days; going into the kitchen yard (out of bounds); climbing the cherry tree (ditto); the possibility of additional food (welcome at any time); fooling around – all these amounted to an unmissable opportunity and in no time boys were swarming up the coal shed and into the cherry tree.

There were at the Dell no formal extra-curricular activities as such: there was Work and there was Games and there was Prep. Any other available time, curtailed where possible by the authorities by means of early bed-times and after-lunch rests, was free time and always spent during fair weather in the woods. And in the woods there were two things to do : one was to make camps, the other to climb trees. The old park had at the time of its establishment some hundred years or so previously been generously stocked with exotic trees, many of them now of some height and girth, looking as if they had been introduced from a Canadian forest. There were several firs and pines, including 'The Tallest' which, though approaching a hundred feet, was actually easy to climb as it had a regular spread of horizontal branches quite strong enough if you kept close to the trunk. All that was required was sustained concentration in the judicious placing of hand and foot, and a good head for heights. Several less lofty trees were regarded more highly by the experts – the Cedar of Lebanon on the upper lawn, for example – and it was from amongst their branches that insouciant climbers would drop fir cones upon the unwitting heads of passers-under, or swing as easily as monkeys.

With this experience and expertise the boys – some already in their pyjamas (quite unheard of, being out-of-doors in pyjamas, but nobody seemed to mind) – swarmed amongst the extensive limbs of the great old cherry.

'Not too many at a time now,' warned Major Oakes, who – judicious move, this, on the part of Mrs Victor – had been extracted from staff supper (a repast of legendary and fantastical quality in the boys' mythology) to keep an eye on things. With his cup of cocoa he had installed himself on his shooting stick in the kitchen yard, from which point of vantage he exercised his own peculiar brand of supervision.

From above: 'Gosh, sir, I can see the top of your head.'

'Drop so much as a leaf on it, Meadows, and it's the firing squad at dawn. And no eating now.'

The cherry crop, which had seemed at first to be considerable, turned out to be enormous. Punnets, milk cans and a preserving pan were fetched from the kitchen; from Mrs Victor's own little gardening shed nearby, a trug. Rather than carry containers into the tree to be hampered by them the pickers commanded the services of catchers below. Though less heroic in its status and function than the commando squad in the tree above, this ground unit had nonetheless its own honourable role.

'I've got two punnets already.'

'I've got a can-ful.'

'That's not as much.'

'Is.'

'Isn't. Sir, shall we weigh them?'

'Hey, look at this bunch, sir. Real whoppers.'

'Give them to me, Dickson. I'd better have a trial tasting.'

'I thought you said we weren't eating any, sir.'

'I said *you* weren't... Umm – tasty – these are first class fruits. Streeter, go and ask Mrs Victor for some paper bags or something – we're going to run out of containers at this rate.'

'Sir!' – this from up in the tree – 'I've got my pyjama bottoms cord caught up in a twig. I don't seem to be able to –'

'Well, whatever you do, Evans, don't let them come down. I should think your backside would make a baboon's look a thing of beauty.'

'Oh, sir!'

Adventurous and skilled though the climbers were, many of the fruits were inaccessible to hand.

'Dickson, go to my room and collect my landing net and my third-best rod.'

This equipment was well known, Major Oakes being in the habit of giving casting demonstrations on the upper lawn and accompanying these with tall tales of the river. Thus equipped, the collectors tweaked many a bunch that would otherwise have gone unpicked, the collectors below wrangling over the use of the net and straining eagerly upwards as if to catch aerial fish. And still the harvest was brought home. There was no such thing – in any sphere (with the possible exception of Mr Bolton's secret shed) – as abundance at The Dell but this was abundance. And it went to their heads.

Numerous containers were overflowing and many hundreds of cherries – in spite of Major Oakes' prohibition – had been consumed by the pickers behind the screening leaves. Nor had the ground force missed opportunities to divert the odd fruit from hand to mouth en route to the official receptacle. And then it wasn't long before the throwing started, it being but a small distance anyway between dropping the fruits and hurling them. It was the dormitories that started it, three of them, in addition to the bathroom, looking out on to the tree. Although well past lights-out for the juniors their dorm windows were thronged with eager faces, alerted by the unaccustomed commotion outside.

'Chuck us some, Clarke.'

'Up here, Meadows.'

'*We* haven't had any yet.'

'I caught one right in my mouth.'

In the tree it was, 'Hey, I got some over their heads in Grenadiers.'

'Try Coldstream.'

'Got that drip Bellinger in the eye – serve him right.'

The branches of the tree shook with the exertion of throwing while keeping hold and maintaining balance. The air was thick with the little orange-yellow missiles and in the dormitories pyjama-ed bodies scrabbled on and under the beds for the fruits that had shot in over their heads. Further entertainment was derived from returning fire with the stones, which could be spat, squeezed between finger and thumb or, by those who had unlawfully taken their cow-parsley pea-shooters up to the dorm, propelled by that means. So from the dorm -

'Got you, Meadows.'

'I'm aiming for Evans.'

'I've hit him already.'

'I bet that stung!'

And from the tree –

'Missed!'

'I'll get you for that, Manners.'

'Didn't even feel it.'

'Hopeless shots, you lot!'

As the shades of the summer's evening lengthened so the

glory began to fade gradually from the scene. The supply of fruits dwindled, failed. Major Oakes began to call the boys to order and command the transportation of the filled containers to official base in the kitchen. The shining faces at the dorm windows withdrew and the collectors in the tree swung to ground with a final flourish.

In the meantime, high in his study on the other side of the school, Mr Victor contemplated no such fruitfulness, for he was looking at the school's accounts. He had also before him the list of those down to enter The Dell the following term and there was no abundance there. In fact there was an ominous gap between the school's expected income and its expected outgoings. In its customary place, in a dim corner of the room, the weighing and measuring contraption, guillotine-like, bided its time.

❈ CHAPTER XIX ❈

Common Entrance was now over; ditto the school exams. There was therefore little truly to occupy the school in the final three weeks of the summer term. In such a climate the plans for a play and the general interest in it were bound to flourish. Suddenly Toad of Toad Hall, begun as a way of engaging 4B, moved out of that lowly confine into a more ambitious project. Indeed it was now being referred to openly as The Play. The interest of Singer Samuel had opened out this possibility. His father, he explained, was a film-maker and this fact alone shot his already lofty standing to Olympian heights. A film-maker! He, Singer himself, however, had no experience of the more traditional forms of drama and was fascinated by the proceedings on the river bank. Very soon he was reading a part, very soon he was participating in the imaginative creation of a production that, already powered by the twin authorities of the Head of School and Miss Beautiful Phelps, now gained the impetus of the New American Boy Whose Father Made Films. A few faint cries from humbler members of the original cast as their parts were stripped from them were swiftly drowned out by the general excitement of the whole project.

Casting became a major consideration and in that sphere Toad was perhaps the crucial role. It might have been expected that an American with all the brashness of his cocky race would fulfil the requirements of the eponymous amphibian but actually Singer, for all his genial openness of character, had none of the arrogance and ostentation required. As far as a home-grown Toad was concerned, self-importance and showing off got such short shrift in an English prep-school that no member of the school had developed those traits sufficiently to suggest his playing this central and crucial part. It might, therefore, prove a problem. Shelving it, however, the co-producers moved on to other roles.

Gay said 'Johnny' – and how he loved the way she called him that instead of 'Clarke' – 'Johnny, you would make the best Rat.'

Johnny was deeply flattered but didn't think it would be right to take that part and to be a producer: it would be too much to do as well as being greedy – someone else should have the chance. So he declined and together they chose Singer for the part. It might be odd to have so English a character as Rat speaking in an American accent but Singer had just the qualities of a clear head, personal presence and purposefulness for the role.

Balmforth was to be Badger. Although not a commanding personality he was quite sizeable and ponderous; he also – alone of the boys in the school – had a deep voice. With a bit of direction these qualities, reinforced by his natural self-seriousness, would enable him to carry off the role quite well. What then to do with Haines – the inevitable Haines? The simple term 'Chief Weasel' was enough for him to indicate his interest in that role, not being familiar with the play, so that was that. One of the competent members of 4B, Morrison, hung on to his part as Mole, and thus the principals were identified, Gay agreeing, under huge popular pressure, to take the part of Marigold, a role originally condemned as utterly wet and unnecessary. Other female parts were easily allocated, as were those of small rabbits and minor stoats, to the most junior members of the school. Some of the older boys with no acting aptitude whatever were prevailed on – particularly where a uniform might be required – to take such parts as Judge, Policeman, Jailer and Usher, not to mention the two halves of Alfred the horse, though the female parts were harder to fill with names like Phoebe and Aunt. In all, it seemed that practically everyone in the school was involved, especially counting in the resourceful Tom Bennet and his team of people-who-were-willing-to-do-anything-practical.

Mr Victor himself was in two minds about this venture. For a start it was unprecedented and therefore dubious; then it was not the role of a fill-in matron and the Head of School to take on the job, normally his, of producing the end-of-term play. It could not possibly be of the standard he himself set and achieved and should therefore not be allowed to take on the prominence of that customary event, now tragically cancelled owing to the departure of Mr Blackstone. On the other hand, something was better than nothing, he was not wholly immune to the persuasiveness of the charm of Gay Phelps and besides even a headmaster cannot withstand the force of a spirit when it takes hold of the community. Mr Denman, a crucial figure in this, was – from the moment of leaning on his mower to observe a rehearsal on the grassy mound – alight with romantically-inspired good intentions on the stage side: one-armed he might be, and in splinters the willow-pattern bridge he had already created, but his heart was committed. It therefore seemed to Mr Victor that it would be best to let the fancy run but keep an eye on it. He had not, however, reckoned on the influence on the project to be exerted – as will be told soon – by Singer's father and Mrs Marvell.

Meanwhile, not absolutely everything else at school had lapsed: there was still cricket, and the day of 'the Banksfield match' came. Banksfield were the big rivals. This rivalry was instigated and nurtured by Mr Victor himself who felt both envy and contempt for a school that, though with only a few more boys than The Dell, was in all material ways superior. Its large old building was of some architectural distinction and was well maintained – the proprietors, Mr and Mrs de Vine having, Mr Victor suspected, 'private means' – its main staircase was massively ornate and the dining room, in addition to a yardage of silverware on the mantelpiece far exceeding that at The Dell, boasted some old portraits and a huge landscape of the house itself in its glory days in the eighteenth century. Its educational facilities were also on a grander scale, having for example a gymnasium with bars and even a vaulting horse like the one deployed in *Escape from Colditz* – the boys from The Dell had seen it and marvelled. It also had a library.

The cricketing facilities were of a different order too. On arrival at the ground the visitors noted not only that the stumps were nearly new and in place at the wicket (instead of being brown with age and put in place by Mr Victor on arrival at the crease at the start of play) but also that there were not one but two nets for practice (a facility unknown at The Dell). They were then ushered into a pavilion where a room was set aside for their team's sole use. Such luxurious amenities might have been intimidating but in fact inspired only contempt in the breasts of the visitors who, setting a fruitless envy aside, were scornful of such softness and extravagance – or 'frills' as Mr Victor contemptuously termed them – and sharpened their competitive spirit. Indeed 'the Banksfield match' was very often a close game, the Dell team, conscious of inferiority in material respects and being therefore the underdog, frequently converted a Dunkirk shambles into a D-day triumph. On these occasions the boys experienced some sense of shared purpose with their headmaster whose hackles rose with repugnance at every aspect of their host's sissiness. Glowering, he donned the white umpire's coat – a ridiculous affectation – equipped as it was in one pocket not with the six stones with which to count the balls of the over but a small metallic clicker invented for this sole purpose, and in the other with the pair of almost pristine bails to be laid on the stumps only at the start of the game. The final piece of objectionable swank was the provision of a brand-new ball – a new ball for every game – imagine the needless expense!

Having won the toss, Johnny put the opposition into bat – a practice favoured by his team since they liked to know what their target was, though Mr Victor was inclined more conventionally to bat first when given the chance. It had to be admitted of him that, though he was hectoring and dictatorial as a coach, he did not interfere during the game. Scrupulously observing the objectivity of the role of umpire he never stooped to – for example – muttering to his fielder at square leg 'Tell Clarke to put Atkins on', or, if The Dell were batting, letting out an aside to his boy at the crease, 'You've probably noticed they haven't got a mid-wicket.' Only when things were going badly could one observe the thunder-clouds gathering on his brow, presaging a storm that would break after the game, on the way home, or back at The Dell, when, excoriated for their sporting derelictions, the team would skulk about the school all that evening, their tails between their legs.

Not that there was much to be done during the game since the procedure was laid down in advance – there was no such thing as tactics. For example, the batting order was pre-set, as were the fielding positions, unchanged regardless of the bowling or the opposition's batting. There was one slip and a third man behind the wicket on the off side, then an arc of fielders running from point to cover-point and mid-off, through – on the leg side – mid-on, mid-wicket, to square leg and long leg. The wicket-keeper stood up to the bowling, regardless of its speed, long leg or third man often having to act as long stops. As to bowling, Johnny and Haines, the fast bowlers, opened. If they didn't do the trick the next two were brought on, though they differed from the previous two only in not being so good. None of them could be described as a spinner except by chance, variation in the bowling coming more from the inconsistency of the bowler than anything intentional. The bowlers' best hopes by far lay in the vagaries of the wicket and the incompetence of the batsmen.

On this occasion the opposition were on good form – in particular their somewhat dreaded ace batsman and demon fast bowler whose run-up was a terror. Destined, it was said, for Harrow, Guy Stuart-Eversley, captain of the Banksfield team, was in command at the crease. Equipped from head to toe with his own personal accoutrements instead of – like the Dell boys

– making do with whatever the old brown school bag might have available regardless of size or suitability; taking a pretentious middle-and-leg guard (instead of the sensible 'Centre-please-sir'); even – an infuriating affectation in Mr Victor's eyes – strolling up the pitch between overs to brush away or tamp down small divots – Guy Stuart-Eversley, with one full and three half-centuries to his credit already that season, was actually as capable a batsman as he was to Mr Victor conceited and irritating and he was now, having come in at thirty two for one, pushing the Banksfield score into the seventies with no further loss.

Scores in matches tended not to be very high. Anything under fifty – though it usually meant that at least one batsman had got into double figures – was probably not sufficient as an opening innings to secure victory. The seventies and eighties were respectable, anything over a hundred pretty damn good, though rare. Today the Banksfield score climbed inexorably, their star batsman laying about him with expertise and gusto and demoralising the Dell bowlers so that even the number five bowler, Vernon – erratic at the best of times – had to be brought on, only to be pasted about the park, the storm clouds gathering steadily on Mr Victor's brow – though not alas in the sky to rain off the proceedings before further shame should be visited on the Dell first eleven. Eventually the Banksfield team innings was declared closed at tea-time, with Guy Stuart-Eversely on eighty one not out, at one hundred and forty one for three. It was not only the very substantial total that intimidated the opposition but the small loss of wickets which combined with the total to suggest a side of unbeatable calibre. Never – or not that season, anyway – had Johnny's team mustered that many runs, one hundred and nineteen being their top score.

It was a gloomy tea-break, therefore, spoiling the pleasure normally taken in the Banksfield repast which was impressive in scope and quantity, including as it did miniature sausage rolls and individual jellies of varying colours in corrugated greaseproof paper cups. The Banksfield side took to the field with alacrity, gaily tossing the ball to one another with anticipatory pleasure, applauding the incoming batsmen with the heartfelt goodwill of competitors who know they're going to win. The heaviness of heart of those two lambs to the slaughter can have been in no way lessened by the warlike preparations of the fielders. Behind the wicket there were not only two slips but also a gully as well as a silly mid-off, as intimidating an array as was ever faced. Then there was the extent of the redoubtable Guy Stuart-Eversley's run-up which was fully as long as the pitch itself; a similar distance separated the wicket-keeper from his stumps so that, viewed from the side as it was by the waiting batsmen, the Banksfield front extended the length of the horizon. To those due to bat – and Johnny was in next – it was a sight to sink the heart. To the man at the crease more terrifying was the spectacle of Evers (as his name was conveniently abbreviated) tearing up to bowl; the longer the run-up of course the longer this fearful spectacle had to be faced. The first ball the poor batsman scarcely saw as it shot past his wicket, then to evade the wicket-keeper and go down for four byes, to the politely suppressed glee of the visiting team who quickly clocked up this surprise bonus on the telegraph. The second ball, alas, coming down with equal pace but much better accuracy defeated the batsman and tore out his off stump which danced along the ground towards the wicket-keeper, one of the bails – to the gratification of the fielder who remarked it – landing at the feet of the square-leg umpire. This was it, the polite reception Johnny received at the wicket seemed to say; don't want to be unfriendly but suggest you abandon hope here and now.

Johnny's highest score that season had been thirty-one not out. He was the best batsman The Dell had but he was not a particularly good one, being both timorous and impatient – that is, he had a rather defeatist attitude but couldn't leave the ball alone if it was within range. 'You don't have to try and score off everything,' Mr Victor had advised him. 'If it's off the wicket and you don't hit it you can't be out.' Any such advice of course went clean out of his head now as Evers bore down upon him. Johnny missed the ball by a long way, swinging mightily as it whizzed past down the leg side; it was nice to have had a swipe, at any rate, and at least he wasn't out first ball. As is clear, Johnny had no high expectation of himself at the wicket, regarding the ball more as a missile to be evaded than an opportunity to make runs, his time in the centre more as a period of testing which he should conclude without dishonour than as a chance to smite the foe. The next ball was straighter but rather short so it was no great difficulty for Johnny to get his bat to it. Rather to his surprise, however, it struck the meat of his trusty willow and went nicely along the ground past mid-off for a comfortable two runs. God – he was off the mark! Not only not out first ball but not out for a duck either! Potential for dishonour greatly reduced. Even more gratifying was the next delivery which, though it came up menacingly high and caught a dangerous outside edge of his bat as he shouldered arms in desperate self-defence, cleared second slip's head by several feet and went for four. Six runs in two balls – albeit four of them flukes. One left in the over. Concentrate, watch the ball. This one skidded harmlessly past, way outside the off-stump and to his own surprise Johnny left it well alone.

The relative success of his first over gave Johnny some heart. Of course a hundred and forty one was an impossible total – even Mr Victor couldn't blame them for not reaching that – so why not relax a bit, take his time and hope that Evers the tornado would soon tire and either begin to bowl more loosely or more slowly or indeed – if he were not taking wickets and was becoming costly – take himself off in favour of a second-rank performer. Certainly his partner at the other end was nowhere near as formidable, being nothing like as fast and with a tendency to bowl short, often on the leg side, a gift to Johnny's partner who took advantage of such deliveries by tucking them away, if not for the mighty fours Johnny was always tempted into, then for twos and threes that made nice contributions to the scoreboard. He and Johnny were beginning to look quite comfortable and had just passed thirty when Evers had him plumb lbw and Johnny was joined at the wicket by Haines.

The latter was not one to be intimidated by anyone and he stood up to Evers with sense and courage which in turn heartened Johnny who was now developing a desire not only to avoid disgrace but actually to deploy the batting skills that Mr Victor seemed to think he had. They both scored well at both ends, Evers' increasingly erratic balls bringing runs in almost every case if the batsman could but get his bat to them, for the boundaries were not long and the fielders were lethargic and inept, more so as the runs kept coming and their Goliath was failing to deliver. But however ropy the bowling and shaky the fielding luck won't hold for ever and Haines got run out on twenty-eight – fortunately it wasn't Johnny's fault – and then the rot rather set in. In a school numbering fifty-odd the first eleven comprises a fifth of the school which means that without juvenile sporting prodigies that team is bound to include some players of little, if any, sporting aptitude. True, the side did not have to sink as low as Balmforth or Edwardes, but there were several players who could neither bat nor bowl to any effect and these now came out to do their bit in partnership with their captain. Few of them lasted long, though Johnny sought to keep the bowling to himself and one or two of them – somehow inspired – managed to score some runs, particularly Vernon – he of the change bowling – who, having been fairly knocked about by the Banksfield batsmen now got some revenge: handling his bat – he was a big lad – like a battle-axe, he made some cracking connections and scored several boundaries before mistiming what was generally known as a cross-bat swipe and getting caught at mid-wicket.

By then the Dell score had just passed the hundred mark and Johnny had comfortably exceeded his previous best : The Dell a hundred and three for six, Johnny Clarke sixty three. It wasn't bad: if it had ended there it would have been no disgrace to the visiting side. But there was life in it yet, and the longer he batted the hungrier Johnny became not only for victory but for personal success. He had never dreamed of scoring a hundred – a half-century would have been a triumph – but why should he stop now? Evers had bowled himself into the ground – that long run-up had taken its expected toll – and the Banksfield side had little other bowling talent with which to challenge the opposition. Johnny glanced at Mr Victor when backing up at the bowler's end: the storm clouds had lifted and a cautious glow was beginning to suffuse his countenance. Was it possible that Mr Victor might actually be pleased? Was it possible that he, Johnny, could actually be the means by which his headmaster might be moved to approbation? Barely an hour earlier The Dell had stared defeat in the face at the hands of those despised rivals; now they could at least hold up their heads if not look down on them. Was it possible that they could actually go one better than that and... defeat them?

Inspired by this wild dream Johnny batted on, protecting the partner of the moment, engineering singles at the end of overs, steering the ball to gaps in the field, leaving doubtful chances. One hundred and twenty seven for seven: Clarke seventy nine. The calibre of the batting thinned out to frayed and threadbare but the runs inched forward, the side held: one hundred and thirty four for eight, Clarke eighty four. Then – disaster: playing a simple straight ball, Johnny somehow caught a low inside edge, the ball bounced off his left boot and ran on to the wicket. One hundred and thirty four for nine: eight for victory, one wicket remaining. Mr Victor's heart must have sunk at the sight of the those two, number ten and number eleven – in a decent side they wouldn't have made it into the team and there was no chance – surely no chance – that they, clueless as they were, now petrified as they must be by their situation, could possibly manage those eight runs. Evers the typhoon, rested from his labours, recalled himself for one final desperate assault upon the one frail remaining bastion of opposition that stood between victory and defeat. Number ten to face the bowling: Evers takes his mighty run-up, if anything extended even further for purposes of intimidation, and hurls the ball in the direction of the batsman who, anxious to do his bit for his side but more anxious to avoid personal injury, retreats to his leg side, down which, as it happens, the ball goes, catching the inside of his bat and running off at high speed in the direction of long leg who, surprisingly, picks up cleanly and prepares to throw. Should they run? 'Yes... No!' The batsmen run, they retreat, they dither. The fielder, equally confused by this confusion, is uncertain which end to throw the ball to, dithers in his turn, the batsmen run, the fielder throws – to the wrong end – it is a bad throw, it is not collected by the bowler, there is no one backing up – more runs, surely – shrieks of encouragement from the boundary rope as the Dell team gather round the telegraph in raucous excitement. In the end it's three runs. Evers is furious, third man is castigated. Number eleven then faces the tornado. This ball is on the wicket, the batsman, astonishingly, manages to play a straight bat and stops it, the ball rolling gently a few yards forward down the wicket towards the bowler. 'Yes,' yells the idiot – the ball is in Evers' hands, he chucks it underhand towards the batsman's stumps but number ten has been backing up with eagerness and makes his ground as Evers' throw strikes home. Fielders in a frenzy, batting side in a frenzy, Mr Victor at square leg frozen with suppressed excitement. Four runs needed. It only takes one ball to make or mar it – a lucky snick can give victory to the batting side, a catch, an lbw, a bowled can do the opposite. Craftily Evers goes for the slower ball, a shorter run-up – less intimidating perhaps but designed to confuse the batsman and anyway he wants to concentrate on accuracy : this batsman will surely go down to a straight ball. Encouraged by the slowness of the delivery, perhaps bursting with the tension of it all, number ten takes an almighty swipe, connects, the ball flies high in the air – Run! – wherever it goes, run! – whatever happens, run! – the batsmen rush down the wicket, their unaccustomed limbs half hobbled with pads too large and the drama of the moment – one run completed before the ball has even reached its acme – it is somewhere between mid-off and cover point – Evers goes to get under it – another run – the ball descends, straight into the hands of the waiting captain, the batsmen now cemented to their creases, two runs completed, watching in horror as their chances of victory fall out of the sky; into the hands of the waiting captain, but – alas for him – straight out again – Run! – the batsmen see, incredulous, what has happened and run again – where is the ball? – Evers looks wildly about him – where did it drop? – he sees – he grabs – he throws – he misses – wicket keeper runs in – fumbles unbelievably – run again! – no, no, stay where you are – the keeper now has it, he's over the stumps, another run would be suicide.

Two runs taken. Score: one hundred and forty for nine. Two for victory to the visitors but victory is still in the balance: a wicket now and Banksfield have won. Evers returns to his mark, perhaps for the final time. It's the long run-up this ball, every ounce of speed and intimidation must be brought to bear upon the incompetent at the other end. He tears in, hurls the ball, the batsman is hit loudly on the pads, Evers – the entire fielding side – goes up in appeal: Howzat?! The home umpire is suddenly the most important man on the field, all eyes are on him – except those of the batsmen who are exercising the one instinct that has been bred into them: they are running, running like mad, running heads down, pad-buckles rattling, bats stretched out ahead of them, tearing to the other end – where's the ball? – does it matter? – just run. The umpire is stolid – no movement of the hand – no raising of the finger – just a slow shaking of the head – fielding side incredulous: surely he was out – only when the batsmen are half way through their second run do they wake up to the situation – they haven't bothered with the ball and where it might have run to for it doesn't matter where it goes if the man is out – but he isn't out – the ball is not dead – the batsmen are running and – third man rushes in to pick up the innocuous ball that has rolled away from the struck pad in his direction – but it's too late – the batsmen are home – two runs scored – The Dell have passed the Banksfield total – one hundred and forty two for nine – the visitors have won!

On the way home Mr Victor stops and buys three bottles of Tizer. The boys drink it straight out of the bottle, like village kids. They burp and laugh. It is wonderful.

❋ CHAPTER XX ❋

Everyone at The Dell was familiar with Mr Victor's MCC blazer, a garish item of great antiquity, its buttons replaced and so not matching, places of tension sewn up anew and even spots of rust as if it had been laid up with old paper-clips, its overall shape having been in no way improved by its involuntary dip in the river during the Choir Outing. His grey flannels were supported by a twisted tie – a fashionable pre-war sporting affectation which now on Mr Victor merely suggested that he was unable to afford a proper belt. The tie itself signified membership, Johnny had heard, of something called 'Izing-gharee' which he vaguely supposed denoted some oriental connection.

For Johnny, of course, there could be no such flourishes to his attire other than, in place of the conventional school one, his brand-new first eleven colours cap which, highly honourable as it was at The Dell, could not be expected to make much of an impression at Lord's, which was now their destination. A suit – since this was a visit out of school – was of course mandatory in spite of its thickness and the warmth of the weather.

On the train journey up Mr Victor smoked his pipe and read the paper with every appearance of contentment while Johnny, officially in charge of their modest lunch basket, looked out of the window. His was not a well-travelled family so the experience was novel and gave him the opportunity to celebrate the glow that still hung about him as a result of the sensational victory over Banksfield, for his noble and decisive part in which this unprecedented outing was his reward. His own triumph allowed him to be a little more appreciative of his headmaster who – though he had in assessing Johnny's innings pointed out several moments when he had done the wrong thing or ought by rights to have been out – had given him public praise. Perhaps, Johnny thought, the old man had got one or two good ideas after all: for example, always banging on about the need to back up and take quick runs where possible – well, that had clinched the victory in the final partnership. And all that tedious fielding practice – if Banksfield had been anything like as good as the Dell fielders they would have saved thirty or forty runs at least, and, as the match showed, every run could be crucial.

Arrived in London, Mr Victor led the way to the Underground with which Johnny was not familiar and they travelled to Baker St which, Mr Victor explained, was, if not the closest station to Lord's, a slightly cheaper ride. It afforded a brisk walk before all the sedentary spectating to come and was the most natural approach to the Grace gate through which they would enter the hallowed ground. The 'grace of our Lord Jesus Christ' was a powerful totem for Mr Victor but Grace, with a capital G., signifying the grand old man with the huge beard, somehow subsumed and transcended that earlier, more remote figure in whose ancient eastern land cricket was of course unknown. 'The Grace gate' Mr Victor repeated in proud and reverential tones, relishing on his own tongue the alliteratively reinforced grandeur of the great man's name and the loftiness of the world they were to enter.

Johnny felt the excitement as they passed through the hallowed portal and made their way to the section of the ground set aside for members accompanied by guests for – Mr Victor had explained – the Pavilion was reserved for members only. He had added that he would himself be paying the Pavilion a visit at some point during the day if Johnny didn't mind being on his own for a while – which naturally Johnny did not. Even as they passed the entrance – glimpse of august staircase, officious attendants – there came a breezy cry 'Maurice!'.

That Mr Victor had a Christian name and indeed that it was Maurice (if such a name may properly be defined as 'Christian') was generally known to boys at The Dell, although that appellation was never deployed, even Mrs Victor calling him 'Headmaster' (though possibly not in private). But it was now used by a man coming out of the Pavilion – another vivid vision (there were plenty about) in orange and yellow with the exception of his face which seemed very red. A hearty conversation ensued between the two and Johnny was introduced. 'Tell you what,' said the friendly man, 'why don't we meet over lunch – bring your picnic on to the lawn.' So that was settled.

'Old friend from the Varsity,' explained Mr Victor as they picked up their score-cards on entrance to the stand. 'In business,' he added, suppressing, in deference to the friendliness of the encounter, that tone of contempt normally present when referring to that branch of human activity.

It being the opening day of a time-unlimited test match – albeit against the Australians – things were quiet in the opening session with only one wicket and some undramatic batting. Between overs Johnny listened to Mr Victor discoursing on the game, wondered how his radishes were getting on and wished he were not wearing so much, for their seats were in full sun and the June day was getting hotter.

Woeful was the contrast between the pitiful basket that represented the Dell picnic and the suitcase-sized creaking hamper produced by Mr Victor's friend, Mr Holland. A wondrous thing, it was, divided internally to accommodate plates, glasses, cups and saucers, with special compartments for cutlery and containers for edibles; leather straps with poppers secured each section. A further basket contained bottles, and more edibles. There was whisky, wine, soda water and even a bottle of champagne whose tinseled and wired top Mr Holland was expertly undoing on their arrival at the lawn. Johnny would not have been surprised to hear Mr Holland, Rat-like, intoning 'It's only just a trifle of lunch. Cold tongue…cold ham… cress sandwiches – nothing special.' The Dell basket – sadly – contained a grease-proof paper packet of ungarnished corned beef sandwiches made with margarine, a couple of chunks of Mrs Bolton's cold bread pudding and an old lemonade bottle of weak (and now warm) orange squash.

'All right for the boy to have a drop, Maurice?' enquired Mr Holland, handing Johnny a half-full champagne glass in presumption of an affirmative answer which was hesitantly forthcoming, even as Mr Victor himself took possession of a rather fuller glass.

Johnny had never tasted any alcoholic drink before. The champagne – that famous drink which he had not seen in his life at the Rectory – seemed to him in some respects like lemonade, being cold and fizzy, but it was not sweet and there was something else to it, something sharp and mysterious, that could not be defined. He drank cautiously.

'By the way, Maurice,' said Mr Holland, now offering Johnny what appeared to be nothing less than a chicken sandwich while himself nobly accepting Mr Victor's reciprocal offer of a corned beef sandwich – 'by the way, I think I might be able to get Peter to say hello to young Johnny here. How would you like that, my boy?'

Peter? Who was Peter?

'Well, I'm sure that would be a great treat, wouldn't it, John?' said Mr Victor.

'He doesn't seem so sure,' said Mr Holland, smiling at Johnny's non-plussed expression. 'Peter's awfully good like that. You'd think he'd be too busy as captain and so on to spare time for a boy but he can remember what it was like to be a keen young' un.'

Only then did it dawn on Johnny that the Peter referred to was none other and no one less than Peter May, the captain of the England side. Mr Holland might as well have offered him an introduction to the Queen – though in Johnny's pantheon Peter May ranked higher than Her Majesty.

'Gosh!' he gasped, desperately mastering his excitement and sipping nervously at the champagne.

As Mr Victor and Mr Holland then went on to other matters Johnny attempted to control himself in anticipation of the promised meeting with the great man. A silent and repeated 'Oh my! oh my!', Mole-like, was about all he could manage. His glass appeared to have been part-replenished and he resorted frequently to its curious comforts.

Then the moment came.

'Would you mind keeping an eye on the things, Maurice?' said Mr Holland getting to his feet with similar unsteadiness to Johnny's.

'Not at all, old boy,' replied Mr Victor with – to Johnny – unwonted conviviality.

After a word from Mr Holland with the steward at the door Johnny was admitted as far as the newel post of the central staircase and instructed to wait. There in the dimness in contrast to the brightness outside huge men, mostly with important-looking faces like Mr Victor's, filed up and down the stairs in a dizzying swirl of orange and yellow and blue and grey and white, solemn and authoritative opinions mingling in the air with cheerful observations. Johnny felt gratifyingly invisible until suddenly there they were in front of him – the gaudy Mr Holland and the dapper, gentlemanly figure whose picture Johnny had seen a thousand times in newspapers and magazines.

'How do you do, sir?' was the best Johnny could manage on introduction. The god smiled, shaking his hand and asked him what was his best score that season. 'Eighty four, sir,' Johnny replied proudly. Then the offer of an autograph was made. Not knowing what an autograph was but feeling that 'yes, please' was the expected answer he gave it, but not having the wherewithals, there was some awkwardness. The great captain smiled understandingly and Mr Holland muttered something about 'being a bit overawed' before thanking his illustrious friend who was then greeted by a more adult admirer and carried off with the colourful throng.

Afterwards, alone in his seat for the second session – for Mr Victor had remained in the pavilion with Mr Holland – Johnny felt some shame at his poor performance in the encounter. Fancy not knowing what an autograph was! And he should have said something sensible like 'How old were you when you made your first century?' or asked him when he proposed turning to his spinners, for England were in the field. Perhaps he should write to him to improve on that poor impression, but to where would he write? Never mind – he'd met the great man. 'What a day!'

It was not long, however, as one uneventful over followed another and the sun continued to beat down, before he began to feel uncomfortable. He had earlier – with permission – taken off his blazer but still retained his cap. Just as he had been brought up believing that to dip so much as a toe into the sea within three hours of even the lightest meal was to precipitate an uncontrollable and possibly fatal attack of cramp, so he had imbibed the conviction (already seen in the provision of bonnets on Sports Day) that to go bareheaded in the sun in summer was to invite instant heatstroke. His head did feel very hot, however, the material of his fine new cap stuffy and itchy, and there was a kind of unfamiliar swimmingness inside it that eventually persuaded him, in spite of nurture, to remove his headgear. He was also afflicted with a thirst which he attempted (in vain) to slake with the remains of the warm orange squash.

Many of the seats around him were now vacant, their former occupants departed to the higher tiers in the shade where they appeared to be slumped, like gaudy elephants, in positions of at least partial repose. Johnny could not bring himself to heft the basket which was still his charge and go upwards in search of shade amongst a herd of somnolent men.

When Mr Victor returned shortly before the tea interval, as rubicund now after his lunch as Mr Holland appeared by nature, he observed Johnny's looks, rebuked him incidentally for removing his cap and found them a place in the shade where he soon fell asleep, leaving Johnny to wonder why this umbrageous resort had little effect on his own condition which continued unnervingly unstable. Added now to a growing headache was a sense of discomfort in the stomach. Attributing the former to the sun and the latter to unaccustomed foodstuffs like anchovy eggs and éclairs, Johnny – inexperienced of course in the effects of alcohol – was disconcerted by the fact that he himself was feeling absolutely awful. In fact he was to his horror obliged to recognize the familiar symptom of feeling incipiently sick. He could not be sick here, surely: Mr Victor would not forgive him. During the tea interval he made a visit to the Gents, locking himself into a cubicle that smelled vile, but nothing came of it. Perhaps he should make himself sick and so be done with it; but he couldn't bring himself to.

It was some comfort to him then that Mr Victor roused himself soon after the tea-break to declare that they should be getting back. They were not alone in this decision – the day's play had not been eventful and the batsmen seemed prematurely to have put up the shutters – so the road to the Underground station was thronged with spectators as tousled and red-faced as they. It seemed a long way and Mr Victor appeared to be labouring and sweating visibly as they walked in step along the gratifyingly shaded pavement. Johnny persuaded himself he felt a little better.

However, no conditions hitherto experienced could compare with those prevailing in the Underground. As they entered the station a gratifying breeze entered with them as if promising companionship – a promise quickly broken as they descended by escalator amidst a press of other travellers. The platform, when they arrived at it, was already thronged and, though they moved to the far end in hope of avoiding the crush, people stood two deep in front of them. In the tunnel – what Johnny could see of it between heads and shoulders – there was an unpleasant darkness, swags of nasty-looking black cables encased in dust and grease stretching into the gloom. Before long, however, a powerful gust of warm air and a promising rumble gave notice of a train, which burst in on them with a welcome explosion of noise and light.

Getting on to the train was, however, a difficult matter. Having waited for a few poor strugglers to push their way off the train through the eager crowds on the platform, the latter pushed forward with barely considerate determination, Johnny and Mr Victor being unable to get on for reasons of lack of space, though they had partially succeeded before being forced to retreat, the picnic basket nearly being ensnared between the inexorably closing doors.

This foray having, however, brought them to the front line of attack, they were well placed for entry into the next train. The front line was not, though, the most comfortable place to be for while it might give them assurance of victory in the next push it put them perilously close to the gaping black ditch through which the train travelled and, more alarmingly, within easy falling distance of the gleaming rail whose current powered its progress and on to which, Johnny knew, the despairing were wont to cast themselves with the purpose of fatal self-electrocution. He longed for the train to arrive but when it duly did he was terrified lest an anticipatory surge forward might precipitate him on to the line, or – worse – smack into the front of the oncoming monster. So scared was he that he even momentarily – but only very momentarily – contemplated the most extreme measure of grasping Mr Victor's hand with his own unbasketed one. Access to the train was successfully gained, however, but there was standing room only. The carriage filled, they pushed down inside the compartment, reaching for straps to steady themselves. The picnic basket annoyed fellow-travellers by bumping their shins, but what could he do about it? There just was no room and the bloody basket wasn't his – in fact did they but know it, these complaining people, he would much rather not have it himself. And the heat was dreadful.

Johnny was not used to this crowding where you stood closer to people than you would in any other circumstances, though he contrived to be pressed against other bodies than Mr Victor's. It was then that he was assaulted by the most dreadful realization: he had parted company with his cap. A frantic search of all the pockets in his stifling suit – awkward and embarrassing in the press of alien bodies – followed by a glance (no more was necessary) – into the damned picnic basket confirmed with a leaden sinking sensation that he had lost his cap – indeed he could picture with agonising clarity his own small action of putting it down on to the ground beside their final seat up in the shade of the stand, could even recall reminding himself, as he performed that action, that he 'mustn't forget my cap'. His mother would lament its loss – it had been new and expensive, and his father would not sanction its replacement other than by subtracting the cost from Johnny's pocket money, which it would take till Christmas to make good. Worse, Mr Victor would excoriate his forgetfulness and require him to write in supplication to the club for its return in the event of its being found, enclosing, in the form of a postal order, an amount that it might be supposed it would cost to send it back to its owner; after which, in the unlikely and unmerited case of its return, a further missive, this time of gratitude and renewed apology, would be called for. It was ghastly.

So ghastly that it distracted him from his own physical sensations which were not improving. So ghastly indeed that he was slow to notice what he could have been forgiven for not realizing was possibly a more alarming fact than both the loss of his cap, his splitting head and his turbulent stomach: namely, the condition of Mr Victor. Strap-hanging like Johnny, Mr Victor stood with his head drooping on his chest like some dispirited primate in fancy dress. Such a lapse from his customary aquiline alertness was alarming enough – more alarming was the fact (Johnny suddenly noticed) that the train was pulling into Piccadilly Circus, the next stop before theirs. Did Mr Victor know where they were? Should not Johnny rouse him in readiness? Supposing they overshot – Mr Victor would be furious – Johnny would be blamed.

'Sir,' Johnny tugged at his elbow in suppressed agony and Mr Victor lifted a haggard visage, the cheery red of his Lord's luncheoning replaced by a greyish pallor. 'Next stop Charing Cross, sir,' he said anxiously.

Mr Victor nodded in an expressionless manner, removed his hand from the strap-ball and promptly collapsed on to the carriage floor – or would have done so had not the press been so thick and supporting hands so ready. Making sure that he had always one hand on something (or somebody) Mr Victor succeeded in alighting without further aid. 'Fresh air,' he mumbled. 'We'll get some fresh air – go up,' and he indicated feebly in the appropriate direction. The long escalator ride dragged their inert bodies to the surface where they emerged into cooler air but a renewed blast of sunshine and the roar of traffic. In more of a stagger than a walk Mr Victor made the short distance across Piccadilly to the statue of Eros. Seeking the shade of its north-eastern side they sat on the steps, Mr Victor collapsed into a sitting position as if dumping some heavy sack and dropped his head between his knees.

'Are you all right, sir?' Johnny quavered at his side. Mr Victor emitted something like a groan and waved a hand vaguely as if to say he was a little off-colour at the moment but would be fine shortly. At which signal Johnny turned, did a bottom-shuffle as far away from Mr Victor as his insides were going to give him time for and, putting his face deeply into Mrs Victor's picnic basket as if in search of some elusive item, was comprehensively sick. Horror at the public shame of his act and embarrassment at the involuntary animal-like noises that accompanied the regurgitation mingled curiously with a sense of release that his dreadful state of the last few hours must have reached its awful crisis and so pass away to give place to one's old friend, normality. He stood up, spitting and wiping the bitterness from his lips with the back of his hand. Anyone who might have witnessed his shame had now passed on, no one berated him for it, not even, surprisingly, Mr Victor who Johnny now saw was receiving the attention of a young woman – a nurse she said she was, just come off duty at the hospital at Hyde Park Corner who had noticed Mr Victor's abject posture and gone to his aid. Mr Victor had 'had a turn', she said, and would be well advised to see his doctor with an account of the incident as soon as he could. In the meantime she escorted him by the arm – how old he looked, Johnny thought – to the kerbside and there hailed them a taxi. In this unfamiliar conveyance they were taken to their railway terminus where Mr Victor paid the massive fare without a murmur (though without a tip), they embarked on the appropriate train and duly reached their home station to find Mrs Victor sitting in the passenger seat of the Morris in expectation of Mr Victor's taking the wheel, only for him to say 'I think you'd better drive, dear.' On arrival back at The Dell Mrs Victor dismissed Johnny with a preoccupied air as she extracted Mr Victor from the car and helped him inside the house. So just as there had been no opportunity for Johnny to confess to Mr Victor the leaving behind of his cap at Lord's so now was evidently not the time for him to make a further confession, this time to Mrs Victor, that he had parted company with the picnic basket, a confession, whenever it would be made, that would certainly omit the precise details and exact location of its abandonment. He just hoped that the sprightly presence of Eros was the only witness to this dreadful act and that there would be nothing to link him to its gruesome contents.

Later that evening, sipping cautiously at the mug of cocoa that was all he felt up to by way of evening meal, Johnny was joined in the pantry by Gay who had just done lights out in the senior dorm. 'Have a good day?' she asked

'You know what,' Johnny replied. 'I think we should cast Edwardes as Toad.'

'Edwardes?' Gay reflected a moment, then smiled at him and added 'Good idea – let's try it.'

✻ CHAPTER XXI ✻

The school was astonished at this startling piece of casting – and then accepted it, Edwardes' poor reputation being unable to withstand the power of the producers in the popular mind, particularly when it was seen how assiduously the boy applied himself to the role. He might be scarcely literate and his handwriting a disaster but his memory was excellent and he was quickly on top of his part. True, he irritated everyone by singing the Toad songs and quoting the cockier snatches of his dialogue whenever possible but at the same time everyone recognized that this trait was of a piece with the part he played and he must therefore be humoured in the interests of the drama. They all wanted to hit him but then of course that was what one was supposed to feel about Toad.

Then – sweeping aside Mr Victor's reservations about the project – came Mrs Marvell. Although the presence of parents at major events like Sports Day was essential and their appearance on the touch-line at home matches countenanced there was no opportunity and less encouragement for any other form of parental participation in school life. The parents' job was to provide the boy and pay the fees, accepting what was provided in return without question or complaint. Mrs Marvell, however, had already shown how widely she diverged from this model both in her personality and in the recent episode of Flop, the pony. Now she was to involve herself again. Learning that

her beloved Max was to be playing a part in *Toad of Toad Hall*
– albeit the very small part of Harold the young rabbit – she
declared her intention to provide the costumes for the entire
cast. Costuming for Dell productions was normally managed by
Matron, Mrs Victor and Mrs Logsdon – a coven that
commanded sole access to the dressing-up box out of whose
capacious resources miracles of adaptation were worked,
medieval tunics converting to Victorian crinolines – and
possibly back again – by way of other different roles as each
year's drama required. When Mr Victor remonstrated weakly
with her – for he was of course still compromised in his relations
with her by her son's involvement with Mr Blackstone, a
potential bombshell that might yet explode in his face – when
he remonstrated with her that creating all the costumes would
be a huge amount of work she laughingly replied that naturally
she wouldn't be doing any such thing for she intended to hire
the entire set – at her own expense, she hastened to say – from
a costume hire company. Mr Victor must remember, she
teasingly added, her own acting past and her connections with
the stage, even though her professional involvement in it had
lapsed the day she fell into the hairy arms of Mr Marvell who
had no intention that his wife should appear in public let alone
do anything that might be called work: she was there to look
decorative and spend his money – a role she took to with far
greater aptitude than that of professional actress. (Not that all
this, of course, formed part of her conversation with Mr Victor
who was horrified by what he knew of Mrs Marvell's husband,
a man rarely seen (thank goodness), being not only unnaturally
hirsute but also very small and wearing rings that did not
become a man, much less a gentleman, whose declared
profession was property developer, a business, Mr Victor
judged disparagingly, of buying cheap and selling dear).

So that was that, the former costume mistresses being stood
down except for purposes of minor adaptation that might be
required. In truth they were – including Gay who of course had
replaced Matron – not a little relieved, animal masks and so

forth being complex and difficult structures to create.

And then there was Mr Samuel, Singer's father. Admitting to Mr Victor on introduction only to being in the 'entertainments industry', perhaps instinctively recognizing that 'Hollywood' to such as Mr Victor was the third city of the plain after Soddom and Gomorrah, it had become known through his son that he was 'in films' – in fact, it was learned, he had to come over to England to make several movies (as Americans termed them) at Pinewood studios, combining American dollars with English facilities and expertise. A prep school production of *Toad of Toad Hall* was, of course, a far cry from the world of *Gone with the Wind* but nonetheless Mr Singer expressed interest, his son being involved, and pledged general support.

Thus the production had established itself not only as authoritatively as the traditional Mr Victor-produced end-of-term play but actually more powerfully now that it had – in addition to the glamorous authority of Miss Phelps – the exotic external support of both the pungently-scented Mrs Marvell and Mr Samuel.

So, casting and costuming having been settled, the producers' minds turned to staging, and here there came an immediate hiccup. The grassy mound on to which 4B, led by Johnny and Gay, had so lightly spilled for their play-reading, attractive as it was, did not offer appropriate facilities for an actual play. For one thing, the fact of the mound itself made it unclear how the audience would be best disposed to view the action taking place on it; for another, it was somewhat isolated in its field so that approaches to the stage area on the part of the actors would be hard to conceal – and then what about scenery itself? What's more, it was far removed from the main building whose protection in the event of rain, and its amenities like electricity, running water and lavatories were necessities when it came to mounting a full production. In short, that delightful original location was in fact quite unsuitable for what was now proposed.

But where else could they go, the Hut having ruled itself out of action? Then somebody said 'What about the front?' 'The front' referred to the front part of the house that has hitherto, except as regards the terrace that Mr Bolton customarily swept each Saturday, played little or no part in this story but is now to come – literally – centre-stage. What is to be visualized here is this: standing on the said terrace that ran the length of the dining room one would look out over the central flight of steps leading down to the wide gravel walk that ran parallel to that terrace in both directions. Beyond that was 'the lawn', these inverted commas signifying something of a misnomer as, although it included grassy areas, it was dominated more by the yew hedges that in rightangular sections gave shape and definition to them and by the central fountain than by those little patches of boy-scuffed lawn. Beyond that lawn, sloping up except in the middle where there was a set of steps matching in position and style that set on the terrace, rose the upper lawn.

In this 'front' Speech Day ceremonies like prizegiving would take place; from the terrace Mr Victor would, bat in hand and snatching sups of tea between motions, conduct his end of fielding practice, the fielders being arrayed on the upper lawn, the ball being smitten one-handed by him over the lawn and the fountain to the more distant area, and returned by the catcher to the wicket-keeper standing at the foot of the steps. The front offered the best play area for juniors, being close to the house, providing, with the hedges, a good environment for 'It', while the terrace lent itself well to marbles and toy cars. It was as close as the school came to having a polite area, it being clearly part of the original with its squared off hedges – albeit now somewhat straggly and with gaps in – shaped lawns and an attempt at a sort of parterre. Not to mention the fountain.

The fountain was enormous, quite out of proportion to the lawn in whose centre it had been placed, the stone basin shallow at the edge beneath its broad brim, sinking towards the middle to a depth of about three feet. In the middle was a plinth that had long since lost such statuary as it might ever have possessed. Predictably the fountain itself – that is to say, its working part of which there remained but a short bent pipe protruding from the plinth – had not operated within living memory. Such a thing would not have justified its cost in any circumstances in Mr Victor's eyes, being without purpose as well as having frivolous Mediterranean connotations. Nor had its basin contained any depth of water except from time to time after heavy rain when a few inches might remain long enough to encourage some aquatic life (including on one occasion, to the delight of the naturalists amongst the boys, some newts) before seeping through the cracks in the bottom, to become dry again and forlornly home to a few leaves and the odd item of litter that the wind had dropped there. On another occasion a fair depth of water had frozen over and sliding was immediately forbidden – though of course the whole thing was out-of-bounds at all times anyway.

'Of course, if that blooming thing weren't there,' said Johnny, looking balefully at the object in question, 'that would make a great acting space – people sitting on the terrace to watch.'

'Sitting on the upper lawn too, why not?' suggested his co-producer.

'You mean looking at it from two directions?'

'Yes.'

'Who ever heard of that?'

'Sounds a good idea to me,' put in Singer.

'Wonderful entrances and exits with the hedges,' added Gay.

'Well, I suppose they can act on the grassy bits, and the gravel.'

'Why don't we fill the fountain thing with water?' queried Singer ingenuously.

'It doesn't hold water,' Johnny replied. 'It leaks.'

'Pity,' said Gay. 'If it did have water it could be a sort of lake – hey, no! it could be the river – Rat's river…!'

'You could have a boat on it,' said Singer. 'A little boat for Rat to row about on!'

'More than that,' said Johnny. 'It could be the canal where

the barge-woman is…'

'…and the horse could pull the barge round and round.'

Suddenly three imaginations pictured the fountain filled with water and swirling with craft and animals.

'If we could just make it water-proof,' said Johnny, thinking how poor the prospects of such a thing were: the cost, the practical task which would be beyond Mr Denman and which even Mr Bolton's inner storeroom would probably not be well enough equipped to tackle.

'I'm gonna talk to my dad about this,' said Singer. 'Say, Miss Phelps, do you think I could use the telephone?'

The telephone! Singer referred to it as if it were as common as toothpaste or – 'Do you think I could borrow your pencil-sharpener?' There *was* a telephone at The Dell, which even Johnny had used to inform his father of his Worthington award, but it was not an instrument in common use even by the staff, let alone the boys. Gay saw the awkwardness of this request and tactfully offered to talk to Singer's father on his behalf, Singer having explained that he might come up with a suggestion if not a solution, accustomed as he was to challenges of such a nature: a man who had overseen the creation inside a large shed of a fair acreage of the Mediterranean sea in a tank on which to conduct the Battle of Salamis might just have the resources to plug a leaking basin.

The news – which took about half an hour to get round the school – that Mr Samuel was going to make the fountain work again sent the place into even more of a buzz than it was already in. This buzz, intensified by the actual appearance of said miracle-worker no later than the following day to consult with Mr Victor on the issue, created an unprecedentedly positive atmosphere, an atmosphere of 'can do' that was quite alien to The Dell. For instance, the question had arisen What on earth were they to do for the caravan – the 'canary-coloured cart' – that it was impossible to stage the play without, Mr Denman had wondered over staff supper one evening.

'Have you tried looking in Mr Bolton's shed?' replied Major

Oakes facetiously, himself amused and aloof from the collective *Toad* mania that was threatening to engulf him.

But Mr Denman had taken him seriously and exploring the domain signified by Major Oakes actually discovered in a shed neighbouring Mr Bolton's treasure trove the remains of a pre-war van. Naturally its engine did not function, being seized up with age and rust; naturally the tyres were flat and perished, so it was hardly a roadworthy proposition but Mr Denman had not kept a Centurion tank operating miles beyond its engineered life-span with minimal tools and resources for nothing and he set about making something of it. The vehicle's chassis he judged to be sound and most of its superstructure; with a lot of grease – the elbow variety included – he felt sure it could be made to move, though that it should be propelled by its own combustion engine was, in the circumstances, too much to hope for. In the script of course, while the caravan actually comes on stage, the offending motor car does not, so perhaps there was no important loss there – though what a triumph that would have been! To the astonishment of all Mr Denman was aided in this task not only by Tom Bennett but also by Mr Bolton who might have been expected to object to this proceeding in his territory. It transpired that his war-time skills – even Mr Bolton had had to do something during the war – were of a mechanical nature and, backed by the resources of his shed and limitless amounts of paid time, he set to with rasp and spanner. The peculiar talent evidenced in his acquisition of so much useful kit in his surprise collection was exercised yet further, and equipment such as tyres, oil and so forth required to render the vehicle mobile mysteriously appeared and were – Mr Denman asking no questions – put to use. Nor, thanks to that same school gardener whose vocation clearly lay elsewhere than in horticulture, was there any shortage of canary-coloured paint.

Meanwhile the recently introduced pony, Flop, had rather fallen into the background of the community's mind. It had settled perfectly comfortably in its temporary home, been fed and watered and occasionally brushed by a rota of enthusiasts, but such had been the bustle of play rehearsal and planning Gay had not had the leisure for saddling up and organizing rides as on that first day of the animal's arrival at The Dell. It ruminated equably, tethered in its field, manifesting little interest in its surroundings unless someone approached with the obvious intention of ministering to it. Boys who were unfamiliar with horses were recommended to stay away since animals – even such small and sweet-looking creatures as Flop – can be unpredictable if treated by ignorant people: a horse was not equipped with hind legs and hooves just for walking.

'Talking of hind legs,' said Johnny one day after a rehearsal with Alfred whose job it is not only to pull Toad's caravan but to speak as well. 'We do have a horse of our own.'

'Flop can't talk,' Gay replied. 'Actually, between you and me, I'm not sure Flop can do anything.'

'Just an idea.'

'We've got enough ideas on the go at the moment, don't you think?'

In fact Gay, if not Johnny, was approaching that period in play rehearsal when the producer begins to feel that the whole enterprise had much better never have been embarked on, that if carried through it will be a disaster and that even if it isn't it won't be worth half the sweat and tears it has cost. One of the particular problems emerging was the relationship between the Chief Weasel and Toad – that is, between Haines and Edwardes. Although the former only appeared in the final scene when Toad and friends come back to Toad Hall to wrest it from the interloping possession of that malevolent rodent and his hangers-on, and although there was no communication (in the script at any rate) between the two, it was not only the climax of the play but one which, consisting almost entirely of 'biffing' and 'banging', is likely to rouse the blood of boys, particularly if, as in this case, they hate each other. While his supporters in that final scene either flee in a contemptible manner or cower ignominiously in a corner to be pressed into the abject service of the restored Toad there is no clear indication of the fate of the Chief Weasel himself. Inevitably Edwardes, authorized to lay about him with his cudgel, would make a target of his old enemy who must – the text required it – run away; equally inevitably, Haines (unlawfully substituting natural authority for the timidity prescribed him by his part) would ensure that before duly departing the stage he would fetch the insufferable Toad a blow to remember; and this could all lead to a fracas beyond the call of the drama that might go so far as to jeopardize its proper conclusion when virtually the entire cast (at least, mercifully omitting the Chief Weasel) would dance round Toad in admiration. Well, only time could tell: apart from 'having a word' with both of them there was little to be done in the meantime other than ensure that no rehearsals involved both of them.

On another front, things were looking good. The fruit of Mr Samuel's inspection of the fountain and his discussion with Mr Victor was the arrival of several workmen seconded from Pinewood studios at Mr Samuel's expense (or at that of his production company) to work its restoration. This was effected in such short order that they offered to repair the operating part of the fountain too but this was turned down on grounds of time and disruption as it would have involved the digging of trenches and the provision of new pipes. When the substance used to render the bowl water-proof had dried the hose was put in and the tap turned on. The filling process was slow but attracted many idle onlookers who, swishing their hands in the water as its level rose, speculated on matters of depth, cubic footage, temperature and how the bowl would serve as a waterway for Rat and the barge-woman. Initial ideas for some sort of skiff for the former and a narrow-boat for the latter had to be abandoned in the light of the extent of the water surface which, large for a fountain, was small for a boating pond and offered little opportunity for aquatic mobility. In the end something hardly bigger or more robust than a sort of coracle was judged to be appropriate, the boat being, it had to be explained to the people, really more symbolic than anything else. Mr Denman made it.

There was, however, one huge bonus and that was that the fountain could serve as a bathing pool. Surprisingly – albeit with numerous caveats and strictures regarding numbers participating, modes of ingress and egress and so forth – Mr Victor gave permission that the fountain might be thus used. So, while rehearsals progressed at any hour, there was always a small posse of boys hung about with towels peering round yew hedges in the hope of their turn for a plunge in the fountain. Though it was hardly deep enough for swimming except in a tight circle round the central plinth this was altogether more fun than the pool down at the hotel which had by now attained its Amazonian river colour and consistency.

❋ CHAPTER XXII ❋

To great admiration and much applause the canary-coloured cart was brought forth and unveiled. The combined efforts of Messrs Denman, Bennett and Bolton had wrought miracles with what, when they found it, had been the rusting remains of a little two-seat open-bed builders' van and was now – well, it could not exactly be defined but it more than passed for a caravan of the stereotypical gypsy type. At least two-dimensionally it did, for it was not designed to be looked at – as indeed in the drama it would not be – from in front or behind. What the artificers in the kitchen garden shed had done – in addition to restoring its mobility which, in the absence of an engine, of course, was achieved by pulling and pushing – was to create two new sides to simulate the appearance of a traditional barrel-shaped caravan, complete with a painted representation of its timbered construction, including even a little window, gingham-curtained, with gaily geraniumed window-box. One side would normally have been sufficient for conventional staging but the producers, having innovatively decided on a bipartite audience, two sides were necessary. This additional work was no burden to the artisans involved since for all of them in their different ways it was a labour of love. The remains of the Hut, even after the depredations of the camp-builders, afforded sufficient hard-board panels for them to bolt on to the sides of the vehicle and although the two panels were not exactly identical, having been painted by different hands, what did that matter since the audience would only ever see one? As a final flourish and as an unequivocal indication (if such were needed) of what kind of love was motivating Mr Denman in his labours he had painted in brilliant red letters against the yellow the simple word GAY. It was generally agreed that never had any production of the play boasted so sturdy and so pretty a canary-coloured cart as this.

It was with mixed feelings that Mr Victor watched this spectacle from the dining room – feelings of admiration and excitement on the one hand, envy on the other. The fact was that deprived of a controlling – even a participating – hand, Mr Victor was becoming restive. Although with its willow-pattern bridge and his own involvement as the leading man *The Mikado* was to have broken new ground in Dell drama this *Toad of Toad Hall* with its innovative staging and props promised to be of a new and higher order. He therefore decided, as his contribution, that he would invite neighbouring prep-schools to admire the show. The Bourne had the previous year put on a courageous outdoor production of *Macbeth* with what appeared to be real swords but its boldness would pale by comparison. That would raise the stock of The Dell on the prep-school circuit. Banksfield could come too and having been taught cricket by Mr Victor's boys could now jolly well learn something about drama as well. And while he was at it why not include Folly Grove, Medlar Hills and St Albans?

Everything was coming on apace. Rehearsals were going swimmingly, so keen were all the participants to acquit themselves well; they had learned their lines and grasped the complicated details of entry and exit necessitated by the yew-hedge arrangement on the lower lawn on whose four grass sectors the action principally took place. (The caravan was pulled on and off by 'unseen' ropes along the gravel path in front of the terrace.) The fountain renovation of course was an absolute triumph and the boating element a true coup de théâtre. Then when the costumes arrived excitement was again intensified as each character pounced on the item labelled with his part and tried it on with glee. Mrs Marvell gave a moral lead to the seamstresses involved in adapting and taking in where necessary, departing with a powerful whiff of scent and promises to provide extensive make-up facilities for the performance which was now barely a week away.

Further interest had been generated by the arrival – again thanks to Mr Samuel – of a sound amplification system together with a collection of sound effects. Tom Bennet was in seventh heaven experimenting with and getting the hang of all this and the school soon became accustomed to sudden noises such as a car back-firing or a cow mooing or an unseen mob baying for blood or even – a popular one, this, but of no application to the play in hand – a machine-gun firing with murderous gusto. Disdain – 'Of course I understand nothing of this sort of thing' – characterized Mr Victor's attitude to things technological, particularly if they were novel, but he was secretly pleased that here was another feather in The Dell's dramatic cap that would put The Bourne in its place with its pathetic attempt at replicating the sound of horses' hooves with coconut shells.

It was all going so well, in fact, that something was now bound to go wrong. And go wrong it did – and in a predictable direction.

'Sir, I'm afraid there's been a bit of a disaster.' This was Johnny at the headmaster's study door, Mr Victor hubristically writing those letters of invitation to the prep schools. 'It's Haines and Edwardes, sir. Mrs Victor says could you come down.'

The sight that met Mr Victor's eye on entering the dining room was indeed shocking. In one corner sat Edwardes, fully clothed and sopping wet, as he had been after the previous occasion at the swimming pool. He was not apparently injured physically – there was no blood – but he was spluttering and sniffing and weeping with abandon and there was an air of total collapse, physical, mental, emotional: he was a Toad completely and utterly deflated. Mrs Logsdon, long-practised from First

Form days in the management of Edwardes' moods and reactions, was sitting at his side, gently dabbing at his dampness with a tea-towel and talking to him soothingly in low tones as to a distressed animal. Haines, by contrast, seemed to have been a stretcher case for, though he was now sitting upright, the central table in the room looked as if it had just been used as an operating table, bloodied swabs, wet towels and the full contents of the first aid box all strewn about with an air of medical emergency. Wearing only his swimming costume Haines, like Edwardes, was wet but his head, from which quantities of blood had been wiped away, had sustained a severe cut above the eye; blood was still oozing from it to be gently sponged off by Mrs Victor, assisted by Gay. The eye was already beginning to fatten and close.

'We need to get Haines to the hospital, Mr Victor,' said his wife in crisp tones. 'This is quite a deep cut – he'll need stitches.'

'And it's possible,' added Gay, 'that he may have suffered some concussion.'

'Is Edwardes all right?' queried Mr Victor, understandably slow to take in the full extent of the carnage in his dining room.

Mrs Victor replied that he seemed to have sustained no injuries but 'I think it might be as well if he were to have a little time at home.' This had an ominous ring to it: during term-time no-one ever went home except upon the most urgent occasion. And to Mr Victor's practised ear there was an undertone in his wife's voice that seemed to say 'I knew something like this would happen: canary-coloured carts, fountains, sound-effects... it was bound to end in tears.'

What had happened? The two principals in this violent drama were not in a condition to discuss it and witnesses to the episode, though quite numerous, did not all carry conviction in their testimony, so differing was one account from another. But the essence of it seemed to be this: Haines legitimately bathing in the new fountain had spotted Edwardes nearby and begun to taunt him, knowing that, being fully clothed and anyway hating water, he would be unable to react physically and would be reduced to impotent verbal rage, which would be entertaining for all present. He miscalculated, however – or had he secretly hoped for this ? – because Edwardes, enraged beyond endurance, hurled himself into the pool in his determination to get hold of his persecutor and destroy him. At first this had seemed very amusing to all beholders but then it took a nasty turn when – and at this crucial point accounts differed (as they will) – Edwardes, scrabbling at Haines, went under. Some said he did so simply in the act of hurling himself at the enemy, others that he was pushed under by Haines, others that he was not only pushed under but held there. Whatever the truth of it, Edwardes had succeeded in exploding to the surface again, in the process hurling Haines backwards against the stone plinth in the centre of the fountain. On this he had sustained the severe cut above the eye and as a result of the collision fallen back under the water, to be extracted therefrom by fellow bathers when he did not appear to be doing so under his own efforts – it was this that led Gay to suspect concussion. The fact was he could have drowned, as could Edwardes. It was a very serious matter.

This episode, while it generated huge excitement amongst the boys, was bound to have something of a sobering effect on the great production for although Haines returned from the hospital the same day, albeit heavily stitched above the eye and with a bruise around it that seemed to deepen hourly and to take on subtle new shades as it aged and spread, Edwardes was gone, not – it was soon understood – to return that term. Johnny and Gay sat on the terrace as the shades lengthened across their stage and the waters of the fountain lay still in the unmoving evening air. (Bathing in it had now been forbidden.)

'Well, now what do we do?' was Johnny's question. 'No Toad, no play.'

Gay replied, 'Get another Toad – naturally.'

'Another Toad? Where from? Who?'

Gay looked at him and smiled. 'You, of course.'

'Me!? I can't...' Johnny would have done anything for her, he would have said – but take on the part of Toad?!

'Well, you know the play, you know the part better than anyone – you probably know the lines by heart anyway,' Gay pursued. 'After all, I can't do it, can I?' she added, laughing.

At which point Mr Victor emerged from the dining room holding his after-staff-supper cup of cocoa and joined them in their contemplation of the scene.

'So there's no chance of Edwardes returning then, sir?' Johnny enquired desperately.

Mr Victor's solemn but unexpanded negative prompted Gay's 'I was just suggesting to Johnny that he should take on the part of Toad.'

Mr Victor looked blank a moment, then said. 'I have another suggestion: I shall do it: I will be Toad.'

A stunned silence followed this announcement, a silence compounded initially of surprise and then of other thoughts and emotions as yet unready – or unsuitable – for expression.

'I know the part well, of course,' Mr Victor continued smoothly, sparing the two directors the necessity of immediate response. 'I have no other involvement, as you know, since the burden of production has been lifted from me by yourselves.'

The fight between Haines and Edwardes which had become such a bleak episode in its repercussions for the play was to Mr Victor a golden opportunity. Even as he lifted the telephone to invite Mrs Edwardes to come and remove her son from The Dell the idea came to him: I shall be Toad. Deprived by mischance of the opportunity to play the part of Ko-ko in the *Mikado* for which he had already been in private rehearsal he was now being recompensed by mischance with the opportunity to play a part, if somewhat less dignified, that was not only sizeable – indeed much the most important in the play – but also rich in comic possibilities. How wearisome it had become year after year to put all his skill into developing boys' skills; how wearisome to see good parts lamentably portrayed, comic opportunities fluffed, tragic moments flattened. Of course as a schoolmaster you accepted this as your lot, that it was for the boys that you did everything – but was there anything so very wrong in yourself being the one – once in a blue moon – actually taking the stage and thrilling your audience with the true richness of the scene, the full depth of the character as conceived by the author in a way that only you with all your knowledge and experience could do? No, surely not, particularly if, as now, he was not depriving anyone else of the chance. True, Mrs Victor had expressed satisfaction at his reduced involvement in the light of the 'slight faintness' – to use Toad's phrase – on the recent Lord's expedition: the doctor had recommended rest which was of course impossible to one in his position – a schoolmaster rested (if at all) in the holidays – rest during the term was out of the question. Anyway, this was a crisis in the affairs of the school and as its leader he must make it his job to meet that crisis whatever the cost to himself and his health. Gay's idea that Clarke should do it was a desperate measure: he wouldn't carry it off at all well. He himself and he alone was the man for Toad: the part was his.

A declaration as firm as this from Mr Victor carried irresistible weight. Johnny's feelings were mixed: at first relief that he himself would not have to do it and then apprehension – a growing apprehension – about his role vis-à-vis Mr Victor as an actor in the play he was producing.

'I can't tell him what to do,' he objected when he and Gay discussed the matter. 'I can't tell the headmaster how to say his lines and where to go and so on.'

'Of course you can. You're the producer, he's an actor: he knows what that means, whatever else your positions off-stage.'

'You do it. I'll just do the non-Toad bits.'

'Nonsense. Anyway, you won't really need to – he'll do and say things as he thinks is the right way. Just sit back and let him do it.'

'OK, but he's not on his own – we've prepared the other actors. I mean, think of the scene with the barge-woman where she has to...'

'Yes, yes, but he'll know how to steer her along – don't worry. Relax.'

But Johnny did worry and was far from relaxed. Of course things would go with a terrific zing with Mr Victor in the part but he lamented the waste of the work he'd done with Edwardes – how the boy had come into the role, begun to enjoy himself and build up a bit of credit with the other boys by the way he did it. Besides, how were the other actors supposed to cope? – it would be worse for them. How could poor old Balmforth in the character of Badger reprove his headmaster for his self-indulgence and irresponsibility: 'You will come with me into my study and there you will hear some facts about yourself.'? How could he say that? It was ridiculous, impossible.

But Gay pooh-poohed his anxieties. 'When they're in costume and so on they'll all forget who's who and just play their parts. You'll see.'

Johnny did his best to be reassured: if she said it would be all right how could he doubt it?

But he was not pleased to hear that Mr Victor had revived the idea, as a final flourish to the production, now – with his involvement – rocketed into the empyrean of dramatic potential, of involving Flop. Alfred the horse was a voice and two characters, each of them now equipped with as splendid a set of front and hind legs (complete with breathing and viewing holes) as people playing this distinctive part could hope for. The barge-woman's horse, by contrast, was a silent one, though the fact that it is instructed in the stage directions to 'put its head ingratiatingly over Toad's shoulder' suggests that it would be best played by the Alfred legs. But Mr Victor had an idea: he was not willing fully to divulge what this idea consisted of but his twinkle suggested that he intended something that would constitute a moment of high comedy that only he himself could carry off. Well, they would see.

❧ CHAPTER XXIII ❧

All then became ready for the great event. While the rehearsal period had at times seemed to drag as if the real thing would never happen suddenly here it was: the performance. All day the school was entirely given over to preparations. Chairs must be arranged on the terrace and the upper lawn – and thank goodness the weather looked set fair, in contrast, of course, with that inauspicious Sports Day when the rain, driving them indoors, had in effect caused the collapse of the Hut – although, come to think of it, look what benefits had unexpectedly accrued from that disaster. But now was not the time for such philosophical speculations.

The dress rehearsal had gone quite well, though the timing of the sound effects – of which there were possibly more than were necessary – had not always been spot on; Mr Victor had not known his lines as accurately as Johnny would have hoped but he improvised spectacularly and of course his great voice gave heart to the singing and the other characters did not seem put off their stride by his participation – indeed the smaller ferrets fled from his threatening cudgel in the final scene with convincing celerity. Whatever little trick he had up his sleeve involving Flop he did not include in the dress rehearsal though he had more than once been seen in private conversation with that animal in its field as if they were hatching some coup together.

A sort of high-tea was taken at an early hour so that the dining room could become the green room; here too Mrs Marvell, true to her word, arrived in good time to do the make-up. The play would be finished before natural light failed so artificial lighting was not required (somewhat to Tom Bennett's disappointment) and therefore the make-up could be applied with more subtlety than thickness. This Mrs Marvell achieved brilliantly, creating the most convincing dimples, pink noses and whiskers on the rabbits who could not drag themselves away from their reflections in the make-up mirror, so impressed were they with the life-like effect achieved. The judge had been supplied with a stick-on beard which he could not forbear handling continuously and the usher with painted-on side whiskers. The barge-woman's face was decorated with a witch-like wart. Inspired by these examples of the make-up artist's skill Mr Victor abandoned the mask intended for him – it was clumsy and got in the way, he said, as well as being rather small – in favour of Mrs Marvell's creative interpretation of a Toad. As is conventional, this more approximated to a frog than a toad, having a large quantity of green in it; the mouth was preternaturally extended into a greedy grin and the eyes highlighted eerily, the hair dusted richly with greeny-brown powder. The whole effect was striking – so striking indeed that some boys found it hard to contemplate the terrifying transformation of their headmaster who, with a tail coat and green tights, presented a figure alarming enough to strike terror into any number of Wild Wooders.

In order to get him used to a change in environment it was decided to bring Flop round at an early hour. Concealed in a convenient clearing in the neighbouring shrubbery he was tethered with a nice bag of hay, awaiting his brief but important entrance in due course. He could be relied on not to create any sort of nuisance or to whinny during the proceedings. The little boat was launched – it had been well tested, of course, for sea-worthiness – and Rat embarked so that he could entertain the audience as they came in with his rendition of the Ducks' Ditty:

'All along the backwater, / Through the rushes tall, / Ducks are a-dabbling, / Up tails all,' while he gently paddled – space did not permit of rowing – about the waters of the fountain, ready to open proceedings with the famous 'There is nothing – *absolutely* nothing – half so much doing as simply messing about by a river.' This interpolated line did indeed get the play going with a flourish – yes, the audience was now seated – just a few last-minuters creeping in, all seats taken – 'curtain' risen, the actors (albeit still fussing at their costumes and hissing desperately for Mrs Logsdon's help with a hook-and-eye here, a garter there) were in place, the producers too, Johnny on one side with the prompt copy, Gay positioned on the other side both for her opening entry in the person of Marigold as well as to be ready to handle Flop when required by Mr Victor.

Gay's entry was greeted with a suppressed 'ooh' of appreciation so pretty was she with her golden hair brushed girlishly behind and a neat little pinafore and laced-over black pumps like Alice in Wonderland. Then when she picked up the daffodil telephone (which Props had so nearly omitted to place on the grass for her) the second of Tom's sound effects was heard – the first being soft background river-flowing noises to get people in the mood along with Rat in the boat – and this time it was the ringing of a telephone. For comic effect Rat picked up from the bottom of his craft an actual telephone (previously invisible) and mimed talking and listening into it in response to Marigold. This got a warm laugh so that actors and producers alike relaxed in the confidence that they had the audience with them.

Some of the smaller members of it – for of course parents had brought younger brothers and sisters along to this 'suitable' play – seemed a little intimidated by the overwhelmingly large, green and deep-voiced Toad and reached for parental hands but they soon relaxed and laughed as the comedy progressed. The canary-coloured cart got a huge cheer as unseen stage-hands pulled it into sight on the gravel sweep and all things went smoothly to the end of the first part, as Toad sings

'Really a most conceited song:

> The world has held great heroes
> As history books have showed;
> But never a name to go down to fame
> Compared with that of Toad.'

In the interval – the actors only with difficulty restrained from mingling in an unprofessional manner with related members of the audience – lemonade (as mentioned in Rat's picnic ingredients) instead of the customary weak orange squash was provided. Johnny joined Gay on her side of the 'stage'. 'Seems to be going OK,' he said. 'Going fine,' she replied. 'Flop still in place?' he asked a little apprehensively, possibly hoping that the wretched animal had galloped off irretrievably. 'Mrs Marvell's holding its head. She's so pleased it's got a part.' Johnny wished *he* was but said no more. Well, nothing he could do about it now. The great thing was, it was all working: the actors were all acting, speaking properly, singing loudly, getting the right entrances and exits, Mr Victor had got one or two of the lines wrong but had recovered without the need of prompting and without putting off the other actors, the audience was loving it and if some of the sound effects were not exactly on queue that was only a minor hiccup. Now for the second and of course final half, then – how could he thank Gay before she left, before they all went their separate ways at the end of term? And how could he tell her...well, really, no, there was nothing to tell her, was there?

After the court scene and Toad's outrageous insult of 'Fat-face' hurled at the judge; after his defiant rendition of his conceited song and incarceration in the 'well-ventilated' dungeon he prevails on the washerwoman through the good impression he has made on her pretty niece Phoebe to exchange her clothes for his and so to enable him to make his escape – only, after a passing encounter with a small family of rabbits (Marvell as young Harold) and a fox in need of laundry, to be caught up with by a posse comprising policeman, judge and jailer whose clutches he succeeds in evading by vocally impersonating a bird in a tree (Mr Victor's whistling here replacing the sound effect Tom Bennett had been keen on), an exploit of which he boasts until, according to the script, the barge-woman's horse places its head confidentially on his shoulder. Cue here for Flop to be led on – oohs and aahs on his appearance almost overwhelming Toad's boastful soliloquy; barge-woman (encumbered by unaccustomed skirts) clambers into tethered craft on pool (representing barge and canal respectively). And this was the difficult bit for Flop: having been led on and attached to the barge he was supposed then to proceed in a plodding manner towards the unseeing Toad who would mistake him for the long hand of the law. Flop habitually did little of his own volition except circle his jaws in the process of eating, and that's where Mr Victor's cleverness came in, for he had anticipated this and precisely in case the pony came to a dead stop on being released – which is exactly what he did – the clever Toad had concealed in the hand behind his back a clutch of horse-nuts which Flop would have scented at a far greater distance than that at which he now stood. He therefore approached Mr Victor precisely as required and gave the unsuspecting Toad a surprise nudge in the back (as it appeared) rather than the scripted resting of head on shoulder. The comic effect was terrific as Toad jibbered abjectly in his misapprehension as to the identity of the interfering agent before coming to and perceiving the situation for what it was and turning his greedy mind to the prospect of the breakfast he has missed. It is here the barge-woman's job actually to feed the horse, which she does with a net of hay that, though inferior in appeal to horse-nuts, satisfied Flop pro tem.

Mr Victor's plan was thus far only half – if that – realized, for the great comedy of this was to lie in his boldly enacting the following stage direction: 'He unfastens the tow-rope, jumps on the horse's back and gallops off.' Now it will be remembered that Flop was tiny, little bigger than a large dog, so that Mr

Victor's mounting him was to be simulated by his throwing a leg over him and standing, both feet firmly on the ground, before running off stage with Flop trotting – galloping as indicated could not be expected – freely beneath him. It will also be remembered that Flop was of a stolid disposition and though he could respond well enough – as already seen – to the 'carrot' form of motivation he was unaccustomed to the 'stick' alternative – not, of course, that Mr Victor employed such an instrument or anything like it but, in 'mounting' his charger he gave it an exhortatory nudge with his knee, accompanying that with encouraging cries like 'Gee-up', 'Go, boy,' et al that should be sufficient to goad the creature into advancing at a fair pace the short distance into the wings where he could do what he liked as far as Mr Victor was concerned. But Flop wouldn't move. On Mr Victor's 'mounting' him he half-turned a barely interested head and remained rooted to the spot, nor did he show any inclination to respond to the physical and vocal provocation described above. All this, of course, the audience, imagining it to be part of the intention, found hugely funny: the more Toad goaded the less Flop moved and the more the audience laughed. After quite enough of this for the taste of all but the juvenile members of the audience Mr Victor determined that in this battle of wills between man and animal man should win. He strove therefore with yet greater urgency but to no more effect. Mrs Marvell, guardian of Flop, after some unseen or misinterpreted signals from the wings to Mr Victor, bravely came on stage, and offering Flop more horse-nuts with one hand and taking hold of his bridle with the other, proceeded to pull. It was now too late for blandishment, however: offended by these insulting attempts to get him moving Flop paid the nuts no more attention than to swipe at them with his nose and knock them to the ground while embedding his recalcitrant hooves yet more firmly in the lawn. Mr Victor shooed Mrs Marvell back into the wings, desperate now to have things his way whatever the obstinacy of his opponent (as the wretched little animal must now be seen); but he had no further resources with which to achieve his aim. Was it – the audience were at first to wonder – an intentional ploy on Mr Victor's part to go quite still and quite silent before sitting down with surprising firmness on the animal's back? Whether intentional or not, it had the required effect on Flop who – as if recognizing at last what was required of him – responded exactly as originally intended and trotted off into the wings, but in the process throwing off his rider who fell over backwards, legs in the air, to land on the grass. Even amongst those who felt that the comic routine with the horse, though inspired and extraordinarily well managed, had really gone on long enough were roaring anew at this comic debacle, little Flop, mane flying, frisking off into the wings, and the pathetic Toad procumbent upon the ground.

There to lie. The audience gradually stopped laughing and awaited the next move. On stage the barge-woman looked on, the words 'Help! Help! The notorious toad. Help!' dying in his throat, while the posse of policeman, jailer et al assembled in the wings in readiness for their chase after the escaping criminal were rooted to the spot. But nothing happened. Toad did not stir. Toad did not speak. And suddenly the quiet that had succeeded the laughter turned to an ominous and breathless hush. Mrs Victor, first to suspect the truth, was first at his side. There she knelt, took his head gently in her hands and raised it: the green face, distorted with its hideous grin, gaped up at her, eyes dulled.

When talked over later – and talked over it certainly was by all present – everyone said they thought he had hurt himself in the fall, perhaps just winded (grown men's bodies are not accustomed to being dropped on the ground even from a low height), or – more seriously – that he had broken a bone. Only Johnny, looking on from the wings, discerned beneath the grease paint a pale reflection of that face he had seen in the tube train on the journey back from Lord's when Mr Victor, his head hung, seemed to be passing out with the heat and the crush. But only Mrs Victor, following her conversation with the doctor after that episode, knew what had really happened here: that, though he had indeed suffered a fall, that fall was not due to any sudden movement on the part of the little horse but to the fact that while still standing and urging the obstinate animal with voice and body her husband had suffered a heart-attack and then collapsed in consequence.

Lucky it was that Mrs Victor, first on the scene, need waste no time in diagnosis. Lucky it was that amongst the audience was a doctor; lucky that the patient was treated promptly and correctly on the spot; lucky that he was taken to hospital without delay.

After the first shock of realization on the part of the audience there was a swift but not unseemly move towards parked cars, the parents of small children anxious to get them away from what could be a fatal scene but anxious also not to instill fear in the young ones' hearts. 'Mr Toad's had a fall. I'm afraid he's hurt himself. We'll have to go home now. He'll be better in the morning.' The parents and visitors – including parties from The Bourne and Banksfield – having departed, Major Oakes and Mr Denman ushered the boys back into the house to get out of their costumes, have the worst of their make-up cold-creamed off by a nearly distraught Mrs Marvell and a very calm Mrs Logsdon, while Gay and Johnny, assisted by the principal members of the technical crew like Tom Bennett, did their best to dismantle and remove all signs of the trivial drama that had now so suddenly soured and turned to tragedy.

It was dark when they finished. Not until the next morning were they to hear the bad news of what had happened to Mr Victor and the good news of his being still alive, so that night an oppressive atmosphere lay over The Dell. Johnny went to bed but could not sleep. Looking out of his dormitory window he saw the front laid out below him as he had seen it countless times before, the yew hedges black rectangles, the water in the fountain now still and glassy. Beneath him – he leaned forward on to the window sill – on the gravel sweep stood the canary-coloured cart, its features clearly visible and the word 'Gay' painted on its side, easily discernible in the moonlight.

❋ EPILOGUE ❋

T he news that The Dell was to close, communicated by Mr Victor himself in early August, came as no surprise to anyone. All interested parties had followed the progress of his recovery with varying degrees of solicitude but an almost equal degree of concern in so far as it affected themselves.

The news was that while – thanks to the efforts of the medical profession and his own dear wife – Mr Victor had made a full recovery from what had been quite a severe heart attack he had been advised that a job such as that of headmaster with all its busy-ness and responsibility was not suitable, that he must 'take it easy', though anyone who knew him would of course be unable to imagine him doing any such thing! It was therefore his regrettable duty to inform all parents that The Dell would not re-open in September. In the hope of a sale of the school as a going concern some exploratory feelers had been put out but it seemed no one wanted to buy a small prep-school these days. Too much like hard work! He was very sorry that so little notice was possible; he had been in touch with neighbouring schools urging them to consider with favour any application from a Dell boy for a place in September. If he could put in a good word for anyone...

Naturally Johnny found himself thinking 'Where does that leave me?' He had been due to stay on a further two terms at

The Dell, getting himself up to a standard high enough for Worthington in the summer. And naturally the staff had an even more uncertain future: for Mr Denman, for example, the school was both his job and his home. Where should he live? – where work?

His decision to sell up Mr Victor did not communicate to the parents: it was another, a purely personal, matter and did not concern them. Besides the issue was under discussion as he wrote. It was not a difficult decision – albeit a painful one since Mr and Mrs Victor had invested most of their adult lives in it – because, quite simply, it was their livelihood and their livelihood was gone. It was not only their livelihood, however, it was their property. 'Who wants a big old house in poor condition plus a few acres of neglected ground?' 'I do,' was, as it were, the response of Mr Marvell, Max's hairy and small father who had become mighty rich by doing elsewhere exactly what he desired to do at The Dell. He explained it all to Mr and Mrs Victor.

The result was that when Johnny paid them a visit some eighteen months later (he had not wanted to go but his parents said he should) much had happened. The house – the school – had, to Johnny's unbelieving eyes, disappeared. The contents – all bar the Victors' few pieces of furniture – had been disposed of, though it could not be imagined that, with the possible exception of the contents of Mr Bolton's private shed – if he hadn't previously removed them – they could have fetched much. He wondered where the famous guillotine, the weighing and measuring machine, was now in use – perhaps it had just been thrown away. The house itself had been pulled down. Johnny thought he'd quite like to have seen that happening, and then thought he wouldn't. He reflected again on that phrase 'World without end'. Well, here was one world that had ended all right – not only his own, but The Dell and the world of the Victors themselves, the world over which they ruled. How did they live now?

On the sale of the property the Victors had wisely sought advice – Mr Victor's old friend Mr Holland, the MCC 'businessman' had proved his friendship in this matter and secured from Mr Marvell what seemed to the Victors a shamefully large sum of money that they were at first inclined not to accept in its entirety, until Mr Holland pointed out how much they would need for their pension and how much Mr Marvell would be likely to make out of it. Which Mr Marvell duly did, the period being propitious for the development of home counties properties now that the chilly post-war economy was showing a sunnier side. The Victors did not seem, however, to have allowed themselves to have their heads turned by this sudden affluence for which they were by temperament and experience quite unprepared. Indeed their house on the old site, number 18 Dell Crescent, was modest in size and plainly furnished and decorated.

Johnny felt ill-at-ease in their sitting room telling them about his first year at Worthington to which, after some coaching in those summer holidays and with Dr Woolf's understanding of the circumstances, he had proceeded in the ensuing September. Mr Victor looked older and smaller, Mrs Victor larger and younger, though they both spoke freely and quite happily. With pride Mr Victor called on Johnny's admiration of the dining table. 'We had it made,' he said. 'Look underneath.' Johnny did so, to observe that the table had been made from the Head of School boards, the last name that of McPherson, his immediate predecessor. 'No time to get you on, I'm afraid,' smiled Mr Victor, who now – to judge by the pile of books beside his chair – was obviously reading a lot and went on to say that he proposed writing, with the aid of the school magazines, a history of The Dell. This, he admitted, was not a topic of huge general interest – he smiled wryly – so it would be privately published but it would be of interest, surely, to anyone who had been at the school and that was several hundred: a readership quite as large as many a commercially published book could boast. He was also doing some coaching in Latin.

Of the staff, Mr Denman had secured a post at Gay's father's school and had become engaged to the matron there. Gay herself was now a qualified teacher and had gone to work in Kenya for a while. Major Oakes was working in a crammer – 'prepares boys for C.E.,' Mr Victor explained – in London and was living with an unmarried sister in Highgate. Mrs Logsdon had retired anyway but worked in a voluntary capacity for Guide Dogs for the Blind. News of some of the boys was forthcoming: Haines had duly proceeded to Rugby, Balmforth wherever it was he was going, Tom Bennett to his 'progressive' establishment on the Isle of Wight; Singer Samuel had transferred to Banksfield for the following year before returning to the States; no mention of Edwardes and Johnny didn't want to ask. Mr and Mrs Bolton still lived in their little cottage in the town, Mrs Bolton doing local char work, Mr Bolton doing nothing (though Mr Victor put that more politely).

Walking home, past the little houses that now covered the Dell's former acreage, he could barely work out where anything of the old place had been: all the big trees had gone, for one thing. Those little houses over there must be on the site of the old Hut for that was the kennels just behind them. Did Dell Close follow the line of the old school drive? Moving on, Johnny glanced with some embarrassment at the cup Mr Victor had presented him with on his departure with the words 'It's the Captain of School cup. Presented each year, as you know. You were the last Head of School – I thought you should have it.' What he hadn't said – Johnny looked more closely – was that although his name had not been painted on the Head of School boards that now supported the Victors' supper, his old headmaster had had the cup engraved: the year, Johnny's name, his period of office. At first he wished Mr Victor had put the trophy in a bag or something – he felt silly walking along the road with a silver trophy. He thought of hiding it under his coat but that would be sillier and so, hugging it to his chest for anyone to see, he bore it proudly home.